# HEWITT

# JAGGED EDGE

# SERIES #1

A.L. Long

This is a work of fiction. Names, characters, places and incidents either are the product of the author's imagination or used fictionally, and any resemblance to any actual person, living or dead, events or locales is entirely coincidental.

Interior edited by H. Elaine Roughton
Cover design by Antonio Stojcevski

This book is intended for mature adults only
ASIN: B01EQ7UHZ0
ISBN: 978-1533012937

# Acknowledgment

To my husband, who has been so supportive of my writing. If it weren't for him my dream of writing would have never been fulfilled. I love you, sweetheart. And to my family whom I also love dearly. Through their love and support, I can continue my passion for writing.

To the many readers, who took a chance on me and purchased my books. I hope that I can continue to fill your hearts with the passion I have grown to love.

A special thanks to all of the people that supported me at SPS. If you would like to learn about what they can offer you to become a self-publisher, please check out the link below. You will be thankful you did. https://xe172.isrefer.com/go/curcust/allongbooks

# CHAPTER ONE
## *Lilly*

His lips were so close to mine, and I could feel the warmth of his minty breath on my face. I could feel the thump of my heart beating against my chest the closer he came. All I wanted was to feel his lips on mine. His body pressed against me. So when he took my mouth, I welcomed him in. Parting my lips, his tongue thrust inside, giving me what I had desired since the first time I saw him. His strong hands began moving up and down my body, leaving me wanting more. Our kiss broke, but only so he could taste the arousal he caused my body. The warmth of his mouth enveloped my pert nipple as he began tenderly kissing and sucking the hard bud. I could do nothing to tame my desire for him. I was his. As his mouth continued its ministration on my breasts, his hand began moving even further down my body. I only hoped that soon he would take me and relieve me of the burning need inside. I could feel the moisture building between my thighs as he continued his assault on my sensitized body. I wondered if he knew the effect he was having on me. My arousal for him deepened with my moans of pleasure when he spoke one word, "Beautiful," before he plunged his finger inside.

"Wait, wait, no, no. Not yet." God, how I hated my alarm clock at this very moment, and just when I was about to get to the good part. It was the same dream over and over. Never getting to where it needed. Only leaving me wet, alone, and in need of release. It was no wonder that my handy butterfly vibrator, which I now named "Max," wasn't worn out. We had a regular thing going on. I guess you could even call us a couple, seeing how we went to bed together and woke up together. For two years, three months, and fourteen days, Max had been taking the place of the one man who consistently consumed my thoughts. I am Lilly Davis, daughter of Lawrence and Kate Davis, strong, confident, and in command of my own life. Not even Peter Hewitt could take that from me. I only wished I had someone to share me with.

As I pushed out of bed, I thought back to what my best friend Dylan used to say, "Everything happens for a reason. God has a plan for everyone." It seemed like just yesterday we were fighting about who would ask Bobby Jensen to the Sadie Hawkins dance or who was going to wear the shiny bracelet we found one day in the gym. That was, until our parents found out, and we had to turn it into the Lost and Found at school. Who would have thought our lives would end up the way they did? Life was so much simpler then. Now, Dylan was married and had a beautiful baby boy named Isaac. I always knew she and Rade Matheson would end up together. I just didn't realize how it would impact our lives. She was blissfully happy, and I was just, well, let's just say... alone. Don't get me wrong. Of anyone, she deserved to be happy. I just wished it was me.

While I was deep in thought about how my life sucked, I heard a knock at the door. It could only be the delivery I was expecting. I had to ship all of my personal belongings here since there was no way to get them all on the plane. I had accumulated so much stuff during my time in Paris, most of which was clothing. A girl had to keep up with the latest fashions.

I wasn't exactly dressed in the best attire to answer the door, so I went to my bedroom and grabbed my robe to cover my cute teddy pajamas, which happened to be one of the first things I bought in Paris. Walking out of the room, I could hear the knocking getting louder and louder. Whoever was on the other side was very impatient. "Hold your horses. I'm coming."

When I opened the door, an older chubby man pushed his electronic clipboard at me. "Sign here," he said, showing his annoyance with me.

"Thanks," I said, taking the small device from him.

"Where do you want my guys to put all your stuff?"

"Anywhere will be just fine."

When the delivery guy left, I couldn't believe how much stuff I actually accumulated. Box after box took up every inch of my living room. Unpacking everything was just going to have to wait. There was something more important that I needed to get done first. I had to find a location for the new gallery. It had to be somewhere that would get a lot of exposure. A place on Park Avenue would be nice, but I wasn't sure if anything would be available to rent. More importantly than that, I needed to get in touch with my bestie.

Walking to the kitchen, I grabbed a cup of java and headed back to my bedroom. Stripping off all my clothing, I headed to the bathroom. I took a quick glance in the mirror and saw someone that I hardly recognized. Living in Paris gave me time to take advantage of the beautiful scenery. I did a lot of hiking and biking. I even started going to the gym to work out. My efforts had certainly paid off. My body was more toned than it had ever been. I liked what I saw. Even my breasts were perkier than they had ever been. Rubbing my hands over my plump breasts, I could feel how much firmer they were. I needed to make it a priority to find a gym, something nearby. Who would have ever thought I would like working out? Looking at the results made me want to go even more.

Spring was my most favorite time of year. Everything was beginning to turn green. Even the flowers were starting to bud. It seemed like there were more people out and about as well. It was as if they were all coming out of hibernation. I needed to focus on getting ready instead of gazing out the window, watching all the people. But before I did anything, I needed to give Dylan a call. Pulling my cell from my purse, I found her number and pressed send.

"Hello," Dylan answered.

"*Bonjour, mon amie,*" I said with excitement.

"*Bonjour* to you too. What has you so happy?"

"Oh nothing, just the fact that it is a beautiful day." It was a beautiful day. I wanted to do something with my friend instead of wasting it unpacking boxes. "So do you have any plans for the day?"

"I was going to take Isaac to the park. Do you want to come along?"

"I would love to come. What time?" I couldn't wait to see my little godchild.

"How about I pick you up in an hour? I need to finish packing lunch. I thought it would be nice to have a little picnic while we're there."

"Perfect. I'll see you in an hour. *Au revoir*," I replied, ending our call. Dylan was always doing fun stuff, like picnics, with Isaac. She said it was important for him to get used to being around people and interact with other kids.

If I was going to go to the park, I needed to change. The skirt and knit top I had chosen might not be the best attire to wear to the park. I decided to pick something a little bit more comfortable. I found my favorite pair of jeans, a New York Yankees t-shirt, and slipped them on. My hair was down, so I grabbed one of my hair ties and pulled it back into a pony. I was glad that my hair grew rather quickly since I had it cut shorter a few years ago.

Dylan couldn't have arrived any sooner. I was so happy to see her. When she told me she was pregnant again with twins, my heart just about did somersaults. It was especially funny when she told me how Rade reacted to the news. She thought he was going to have a heart attack. I had never seen her so happy. When the day came for me to be a mom, I hoped that I would be a good mom just like her.

It was a short drive to Central Park. The park was always busy on Saturdays. It seemed like everyone in Manhattan was there. Since the park was so big, it wasn't hard to find a place to set up for our picnic. Isaac spotted the children's playground right away. He was so cute the way he kept tugging on my arm to take him to the play area.

"Nant Illy, come, come," he said with excitement, pulling my arm with everything he had.

"I'm coming, little guy," I said as he pulled me towards the playground. I never knew a child could be so strong.

While Dylan was setting up the picnic area, Isaac and I played. Isaac tried to convince me that I needed to go on the jungle-gym with him. No way was going to happen. Instead, I pointed him to the swing set and offered to push him while he swung. It was an easy trade considering he loved to swing.

By the time we finished playtime, I was exhausted and starving. Dylan already had everything laid out for us. She always thought of everything. She had our place settings perfectly placed on the picnic table, along with more than enough food. Dylan made ham and cheese sandwiches for us, while little Isaac had peanut butter and jelly. She also brought fruit and chocolate chip cookies. I was hoping that the chocolate cookies were for me. What's the fun in eating fruit, unless it happened to be the grape kind served in liquid form?

We had so much fun at the park that we really didn't get much of a chance to really talk to one another. Isaac kept us both busy with the playground as we alternated in taking him. It was approaching two o'clock when Isaac finally had enough. He ended up falling asleep on the blanket that Dylan had spread out on the grass. She gathered Isaac in her arms while I gathered everything else. He didn't even stir when she picked him up. He was out.

On the way home, Dylan suggested I come to her house for a while. She thought we could catch up while Isaac took a nap. I hadn't spent any real girl time with anyone in such a long time. I couldn't pass up the opportunity with my BFF. We had so many things to catch up on. The last time I spent any time with Dylan was the night her life fell apart.

When she told me Rade was taking her to this sex club, I tried to convince her it was a bad idea. It was funny how things turned out. She managed to get past what happened to her. Now it's a weekly thing for them. Not too sure how on board I was with this weekly "date night," but it seems to be working for them. Still, I would like to know how it fits into their lives, especially with little Isaac in the picture.

# CHAPTER TWO
## *Lilly*

Maria took little Isaac while Dylan and I settled on the back patio. When Dylan told me that Rade had found the perfect home for them on the outskirts of New York, I wasn't thrilled about being so far away from my friend. Even though I was still living in Paris, I knew that I would be returning to New York and living here permanently. Call it selfishness, but I wanted to have my best friend close to me. I didn't want to waste any time driving to be with her, especially if I needed her when I was having an emotional breakdown, which I was having a lot of lately.

"So how are things with you since you moved back to the States?" Dylan asked, pulling me from my thoughts.

"Pretty good, actually. All of my things arrived this morning from Paris. I still need to find a place for the new gallery, but other than that, really good." I shifted slightly in my seat, hoping that my answer satisfied her question.

"That's not what I meant, Lilly. I was referring to you and Peter. Have you seen him yet?" Dylan asked, smiling as she handed me a glass of ice tea.

One thing about my friend, she could be direct and to the point at times. I shouldn't have been surprised, though. I didn't give Dylan any reason to believe that my relationship with Peter was over. All she knew was that we had gone our separate ways when I moved to Paris. Now that I was back, it only seemed reasonable that we would hook up again. "I haven't seen Peter. To be quite honest, I'm not sure if I want to see him. We didn't end things with the best of terms when I left."

"I just thought you guys would be able to work things out now that you're back on a permanent basis. He still asks about you," Dylan confessed.

"What do you mean he still asks about me?" I shouldn't have cared, but deep down, I thought about Peter more than I should have. Even though things between us ended badly, there wasn't a day that went by that I didn't think about him. He was the only man who could make me feel things that I had never felt before. I wasn't by no means inexperienced, but some of the things he did to me, well, let's just say, you couldn't learn them from a self-help book.

"He still cares about you, Lilly. I really think he feels bad about the way things ended between you two. I'm not telling you what to do, but you should think about talking to him. Give him another chance."

Maybe Dylan was right. Everyone had secrets. Look at her life with Rade. He had enough secrets for the entire population of Manhattan. Everything worked out for them. She had a beautiful home, a beautiful little boy, and a man who loved her more than anything. "I'll think about it," I replied. I just wasn't sure if I was ready to get my heart broken again.

Dylan grabbed my hand and gave it a gentle squeeze, signaling her appreciation. "So what is this about a new gallery?"

I was thankful that she had changed the subject. As I told her what my plans were, her eyes lit up with excitement. I almost believed she was more excited than I was. She even offered to have Maria watch Isaac while we looked for a spot for the gallery together. Dylan even went as far as offering to help me name it.

"I almost forgot," Dylan blurted out. "We are having a grand opening for Tetralogy. I want you to come."

"I wouldn't miss it for the world, Dylan. Let me know when and where, and I'll be there." I knew how important this was for Dylan. She worked so hard to get the new facility up and running. At first, she wasn't sure she would be able to run the new company Rade had purchased. I knew she would make it a great success, mostly since everyone wanted the latest in new software to make their lives easier.

"It's a couple of weeks away, but it will be at the new site. I'm very hopeful that there will be a lot of people there," Dylan said.

"Knowing you, my friend, it will be a hit," I giggled, lifting my glass in a toast.

~****~

By the time Richard took me back to my condo, it was dinner time. Dylan had offered for me to stay, but I knew boxes were waiting for me to unpack. I wished I had taken her up on her offer. When I opened the door, I was hit with twenty-plus boxes needing to be unpacked. I wasn't sure where I was going to start, but first things first. If I was going to tackle these boxes, I was going to do it in comfortable clothing. Heading to my bedroom, I took in a deep sigh of regret. "This is not how I planned on spending a Saturday night. Then again, what kind of plans did I really have?"

It was well past midnight, and I had only unpacked a quarter of the boxes in my living area. I decided to call it quits and opted for a nice hot bath. There was nothing like a mound of bubbles to soothe an achy body, a body in dire need of some TLC. As I lay in the tub, I began thinking about what Dylan said about reaching out to Peter. Even though things didn't end well, he hadn't left my mind since the day I told him it would be better if we went our separate ways. As much as it hurt, I could never bring myself to delete his number from my phone. There were so many times I thought about calling him just to say "Hi." In the end, I always chickened out and did nothing. Maybe tomorrow morning would be different. Maybe I would be able to actually hit the little green phone icon instead of just staring at it.

# CHAPTER THREE
## *Lilly*

The morning came too soon. It was 6:00 a.m., and I knew that if I wanted to do something other than unpacking boxes, I needed to get started on it. Stumbling out of bed, I went to the bathroom, did my thing, and headed to the kitchen for some much-needed coffee. After having the first taste of my morning pick-me-up, I began digging into the remaining boxes. Most of the boxes were filled with clothing, so I saved those for another time. I did manage to carry them to the bedroom to make more room in the living area. I finally felt like I was making progress. The shaggy white rug I had over the wooden floor was finally visible.

When I emptied the last box of its contents, it was nearly 10:00 a.m. I was glad I hadn't wasted my whole day unpacking. Most importantly, I had plenty of time to check out the new gym I saw around the corner from my building. I was glad that the old empty building finally turned into something useful and not one of those organic markets containing stuff nobody heard of. Changing into my workout clothes, I decided to call Dylan to see if she wanted to tag along with me.

"Hey, girlfriend," I began, "Whatcha doing?"

"Usually, when you ask me what I'm doing, it means you either want something or you want me to go with you somewhere." Dylan knew me too well. When you know each other for more than fifteen years, you tend to get to know someone pretty well.

"I was going to check out the new gym that opened up around the corner from me. I thought maybe you would want to go with me," I ask, hoping she would accept.

"I would love to go with you. Give me about an hour. I just need to get Isaac settled, and I'll be over."

"Perfect."

While I waited for Dylan to show up, I thought I would occupy my time looking for a real estate agent. Searching the Web, I found one who specialized in commercial properties. I emailed her what I was looking for, and she instantly emailed me back with some listings close to the area I wanted. After looking at the listings, I was beginning to have second thoughts about her. Some of the listings she shared were complete dumps. I could tell just by looking at the pictures. The buildings that weren't, were either too small or so outrageously priced it was no wonder they hadn't sold yet. By the time I got off the phone with her, I could tell she was annoyed with me. It didn't really matter. If I was going to pay a sizable amount for a spot, then she could be as annoyed as she wanted to. I wasn't about to get talked into something I didn't like.

Just as I was finishing up with the realtor, a knock came at the door. Looking through the peephole, I could see it was Dylan. Even though it had only been yesterday since I'd seen her, I really missed her. So when my greeting ended in a big hug, it threw her a little off guard.

"I guess you're glad to see me," she said with a smile.

"I just really missed you." It was the truth. I might have gone a little overboard, though.

I grabbed my bag, and we headed to the new gym, only it wasn't really new, in the sense that it had been there for a year and a half. I had missed so much while I was gone.

Since it was a gorgeous day, we decided to walk. One thing about New York, you never knew what to expect when it came to the weather. It could be unseasonably warm one day and a blizzard the next.

When we entered the gym, I could tell it was a popular place. Looking around, I could see that several classes were going on in various rooms. The main room where most of the exercise equipment was located had people doing their own thing. As we walked up to the reception area, there was no one around. Dylan picked up the bell sitting on the counter and began ringing it. Within seconds, a very fit guy came to assist us.

"Good afternoon, ladies, is there something I can help you with?" he greeted us in a friendly manner.

"Yes, we would like some information on joining the gym," I replied.

"I think I can help you out with that," he smiled as he pulled several forms from behind the counter.

An hour later, we were signed up as members. I couldn't believe how much the gym had to offer for the monthly membership fee. It had several classes ranging from low-impact aerobics to high-intensity kickboxing. There was even a special class offered to soon-to-be mothers. This was what sold Dylan. She was all about being as healthy as possible during her pregnancy.

As we were leaving, we were so excited about joining that I didn't notice the man walking into the gym. I would have fallen on my ass hadn't it been for his arms reaching out for me. Looking up at him, I couldn't help but stare. He was very handsome.

"I'm so sorry," I said, blushing from embarrassment. "I should watch where I'm going."

"No need to apologize. I should have been paying more attention," he said in a deep voice.

As Dylan and I stepped outside, Dylan gave me one of those 'Are you crazy' looks? I knew that look and what she was thinking.

"Don't say anything, Dylan. I know what you're thinking." I didn't want her to know that I was at a loss for words. I was too busy, staring at his incredible body. Hopefully, I would have another chance to get to know him better.

When we got to my building, Dylan decided she needed to get back home to Isaac. I knew it was hard for her to leave him for any length of time, and she had already been away from him for a couple of hours. It was a good thing that she made sure that Tetralogy had a daycare center on-site; otherwise, she would have never agreed to keep working.

Before she left, we decided to meet up again on Wednesday to go to the gym. Wednesdays and Fridays were the two days they offered the low-impact classes for expecting mothers.

Getting off the elevator, I could tell there was something wrong. The door to my condo was open, and I could have sworn that I locked the door when Dylan and I left. Grabbing the pepper spray from my bag, I held it up in front of me as I slowly pushed the door open. Looking inside, I saw that no one was there. I slowly walked through the door when I heard a noise coming from down the hallway. It sounded like the noise was coming from the bathroom. My grip tightened around the bottle of pepper spray as I approached the bathroom door. As I pushed the door open, a white and gray fur-ball appeared before me. "Oliver, what are you doing here?" I asked, thinking the cat would somehow be able to answer me. Taking a deep breath, I put the spray back in my bag and picked up the overweight Siamese cat.

Walking out of my place down two doors to Mrs. Jensen's, I held on to Oliver as I knocked on the door. Mrs. Jensen opened the door with a big smile on her face. I knew how much she loved that cat. What I couldn't understand was how he managed to get out? Mrs. Jensen always made sure he never went outside her home. Mrs. Jensen thanked me for returning Oliver. I really wasn't a cat person, but Oliver was beginning to grow on me.

~****~

By the time Wednesday rolled around, I was ready for a good workout. Natalie, my real estate agent, showed me some more buildings for my gallery. Everything she showed me wasn't even close to what I wanted. It was mostly the same thing, either too small or too pricey. So when Dylan called and asked if she could meet me at the gym, I was all for it. This meant I could leave a little earlier and get rid of some of the stress I was carrying.

Entering the building, I could see that everyone was pretty much as they were the first time we came. I thought a good warm-up would get me on my way to release some of the tension I had. I decided to start with a couple of miles on the treadmill. Dylan showed up just as I was finishing up. Her class was just about to start, so I headed back to the weight area and decided to work on my upper body. As I looked around, I wondered about the good looking guy I plowed into a couple of days ago. I was kind of disappointed when I didn't see him.

Dylan was finished with her class about an hour later, looking like she really enjoyed herself. I still wanted to work on my lower body, so we decided to meet up again next Wednesday. Dylan didn't want to overdo her first week. The last thing she wanted was to be sore and pregnant.

# CHAPTER FOUR
## *Lilly*

I couldn't believe the way my body felt the next morning. Every muscle hurt. Even muscles I didn't know I had hurt. It felt like I competed in a triathlon. I needed to do something to loosen up. The first thing I needed was to get some pain reliever. Stumbling out of bed, I headed to the medicine cabinet in my bathroom for my relief. I popped two ibuprofen tablets into my mouth and waited for them to kick in. An hour later, there was still no relief. I decided maybe a walk would help loosen my tight muscles. Putting on my favorite Nikes, I headed out the door for Central Park.

It was another beautiful day with even more people taking advantage of the nice weather. Just as I stepped across the street, I felt the vibration of my cell phone. I was hoping it was the realtor letting me know she had found a place. When I looked down at my screen, I didn't recognize the number. I went ahead and answered it, just in case it was the real estate agent. Greeting the caller with a "Hello," I waited for a response. There was only silence on the other end. Before I could say "Hello" again, the caller hung up. Whoever it was must have realized they had the wrong number. Thinking nothing of it, I slipped my phone back into my pocket and proceeded to the park.

Walking for about half an hour, I could feel the tension in my muscles begin to ease. I was just about ready to head back to my condo when another call came in on my cell. This time it was Natalie, my real estate agent. "Hey, Natalie," I said as I continued walking.

"Hey, Lilly, sorry to call you so early, but I think I may have found the perfect spot for your gallery. It's in a perfect location," she said with excitement.

Hailing a cab, I gave the driver directions to where I needed to go. The address Natalie provided me was just off of 5th Avenue, near the Garment District. I didn't think there were any buildings available on that side of town, but it made me happy that Natalie found something. It was a perfect area with lots of foot traffic.

As the driver pulled up to the curb, I could see Natalie waiting in front of a dark brick building. I paid the cab fare and stepped onto the curb. The building's curb appeal was pretty impressive, with its glass front and huge ceramic pots, filled with greenery, on each side of the double glass doors. If the inside were anything like the outside, it would be the perfect place.

Natalie unlocked the double glass doors, and we stepped inside. The main floor was massive. It must have been at least 4000 square feet of open space. I pictured, in my mind, how it would look with all the artwork I had stored. I could see room for a sizable office and a conference room. Natalie pointed to a set of stairs situated to the right of the room. I could tell that they led to a second floor with a long balcony that overlooked the main floor. Everything was perfect about the building: the location, the size, everything.

By the time we left, I had signed a contract to purchase the building. Natalie assured me there was no way the buyer would turn down my offer, especially since I offered more than what they were asking for. I was so excited; I had to share my excitement with Dylan.

~****~

Rade was out of town on business for a couple of days, so when I told Dylan about my great news, she suggested I stay with her until he got back. Unable to turn her down, I made plans to visit her for a couple of days. I packed a small bag and waited for Richard to pick me up.

Dylan insisted that Richard pick me up since it was her invitation. A sleek black Bentley pulled up to the curb just as I exited my building. Being the gentleman that he was, Richard got out of the car and assisted me with my bag, then opened the passenger door for me to get in.

"Hello, Richard. It's been a while," I said with a smile.

"It has, Ms. Davis," he replied with the tip of his head.

The ride to Dylan's was quiet. I was mostly thinking about all the possibilities of what could be done to the new place for my gallery. My mind was filled with so many ideas that I couldn't wait until it became a reality.

When we got inside the house, Maria was waiting at the front door to greet us. She let me know that Dylan was in the living area playing with Isaac. Richard took my bag to the guest room upstairs while I went to the living room. Dylan and Isaac were playing on the floor. Watching them together made my heart sing. There was nothing like the love Dylan had for Isaac. Isaac must have heard me because he turned his little body and jumped from the floor.

"Nant Illy," he said with excitement as he leaped into my arms.

"Hey, little guy," I said, holding him close to me.

"Me and Mommy are making a house. Come see, Nant Illy, come see," he whispered, pulling me toward a house made with playing cards.

I knew he was trying to be quiet so that the cards wouldn't tumble. I followed him slowly to where Dylan was sitting on the floor. The stacked cards were three stories high. I was amazed at how well he was doing as his tiny hands grabbed a card and carefully placed it on the card house. When he looked back over to me with a smile, I knew he was up to something. His little body lunged at the neatly stacked cards, and one by one, the cards tumbled to the floor. Dylan looked at me and then at Isaac. Isaac covered his mouth with his little hand and began laughing. Soon we were all laughing.

Maria must have thought we lost our marbles, the way she was standing at the entrance. In a soft voice, she said, "I'm ready to take off. Would you like me to put Isaac to bed before I leave?"

"That would be wonderful, Maria," Dylan said as she stood and lifted Isaac from the floor, handing him to Maria.

I stood and headed to the patio with Dylan while Maria took Isaac to bed. The night was still warm, and Dylan thought it would be nice to have a drink under the stars. She, of course, had sparkling water, while I had a glass of wine. As we took our seats, I thought back to when we were in college and how we used to share our most intimate thoughts while looking at the stars. So many things had changed since then.

Dylan grabbed my hand, pulling me from my thoughts. Looking over to her, I could see that tears were beginning to form in her eyes. Something must have set it off. "What's going on, Dylan?" I asked.

"There's something that I need to say. It's about what happened the day Michael died," Dylan began, wiping away the tears from her face. "I've never been able to share with anyone how I really felt."

"It will be okay, Dylan. Everything will be okay," I said, pulling her close to my side.

Looking back, I remember how angry she was at me for introducing her to Michael, even though they ended up together. They were so happy together, even planned to get married. They were meant to be together, or so I thought. Who would have thought that he would end up being someone capable of staging his own death and stealing millions from the man Dylan loved more than life itself?

"I feel like I was the reason he didn't fight for his life. He told me that he no longer had to hurt and that he always loved me. I never told anyone, not even Rade. Why didn't he just give up when he had the chance?"

As I continued to listen to Dylan, I could tell she had a lot weighing on her mind. Who knew how long this had been tormenting her? I didn't know the full story as to what had happened to her. I only knew that Michael had kidnapped her with the help of Rade's ex, Chloe Dupree, who was totally wacko. She was obsessed with Rade. They had a history together, and Chloe wasn't about to let anything stand between them. She even went as far as to get pregnant from him. She was psycho with a capital P. Somehow, Michael got shot during the rescue, and Chloe got away. I only heard later how she came after Dylan with a vengeance. If she couldn't have Rade, nobody could. That was the day I almost lost my best friend to that crazy woman. Thank God, Chloe was locked away for good.

Looking at my friend, I gave her what she needed. "I'm not sure what you're thinking, Dylan, but stop. This whole thing, as demented as it was, was never your fault. Michael caused his own fate. He was responsible for his own actions. Not you or anyone else for that matter. So stop thinking it was your fault or that you could have prevented what happened." I might have been overly candid with her, but she needed to know that by no means was it her fault.

I wasn't sure how long Dylan and I talked, but it felt good to talk to her. Even though we kept in touch while I was in Paris, it was never the same as being right here with her. She was my best friend, and I loved her like a sister.

# CHAPTER FIVE
## *Lilly*

I thought my own bed was the most comfortable bed on earth. I was wrong. The bed I was currently lying in made me never want to get up. I had to let Dylan know that unless she wanted me to move in with her, she better get rid of that bed.

Regretting that I needed to get up, I slowly climbed out of heaven and padded to the bathroom. After doing what I needed to do, I headed down the staircase in need of some caffeine. About halfway down the stairs, the aroma of Columbian coffee filled my nose. As I reached the bottom, I heard voices coming from the kitchen. One voice I recognized as Dylan's, but the other was male, and I knew it wasn't Rade since he was still gone. It wasn't Richard, either. The voice I was hearing was much younger. As I got closer to the kitchen, it was a young man Dylan was talking with. I only saw his back, but from what I saw, he was in very good shape. He was also quite tall. If I had to guess, I would say around six feet. He had thick blonde hair and a very well-built body. Just as I was about to say something, he turned my way.

"Lilly, you're awake. How about some coffee?" Dylan asked as she began pouring coffee in a mug.

"You read my mind." Even though I needed my morning coffee fix, I needed to know who this cute guy sharing a cup of coffee with me was. At least, he was in my eye. "And who might you be?"

"I'm sorry, Lilly. I forgot you hadn't met Rade's brother," Dylan said. "Evan Taylor, meet Lilly Davis."

His eyes were focused on me. I could see the resemblance, especially in the eyes. It wasn't until I looked away from him that I realized the reason for his interest in me. I wasn't exactly wearing the right clothing for an introduction. "If you'll excuse me, I need to shower." As quickly as I came, I went. It wasn't one of my greatest moments, more like embarrassing, to say the least. Backing away until I was out of view, I ran up the stairs.

By the time I finished showering, Evan was already gone. I would have loved to visit with him more, but it was probably better that he left. I didn't know if I could face him knowing what impression I made on him being half-naked. Dylan was no longer in the kitchen either. I stepped out onto the patio to find that she and Isaac were outside. I watched them play ball for a few minutes before I went down the few steps from the patio to the plush green lawn they were playing on.

"Hey, you two! You look like you're having fun," I said.

"I was just about to check on you," Dylan said as she threw the large ball to Isaac. "I thought we would go shopping for the grand opening of Tetralogy. I can't exactly fit into anything I have."

Even though Dylan was only a couple of months pregnant, I could tell that she had gained a few pounds. I also noticed that she was eating a lot more than she usually did. I guess that's what happens when you are going to have twins. "I would love to go shopping with you. You know me."

"Yeah, how could I forget the last time we went on a shopping spree? My feet were sore for a week."

"It wasn't that bad, Dylan. Besides, I remember that knock-out dress you bought. If I remember correctly, it was the night you and Rade got back together."

~****~

We must have shopped at twenty different stores before Dylan finally found the perfect dress. Being pregnant and married, she went for a more conservative look. The dress she chose was still very elegant, and it fit her perfectly. I, on the other hand, chose something a little less conservative but still tasteful. After shopping all morning, we decided to have lunch at a small café up the street from where Dylan had found her perfect dress.

After a perfect lunch, Dylan dropped me off at my place. I hadn't been to the gym in a couple of days, and I needed to work off the lunch I had just consumed. As I was changing into my workout clothes, my cell began to ring. Taking it from my purse, I saw it was an unknown number. It was bizarre that I was getting these calls from the same number. Answering the call, just like before, I was greeted with silence. And just like before, I hung up. I swore that if I received another call from this number with no response, I would use every word in the profanity dictionary.

Entering the gym, it was once again hopping. I did my usual two-mile run on the treadmill before I headed to the weight room. Entering the room, which seemed like only men used, I wasn't prepared for who greeted me as I entered.

"Funny seeing you here. How have you been, Lilly?" Peter looked good. As a matter of fact, he looked perfect.

"Um... Hi...," I stuttered, trying to compose my reaction to his hard body. I wasn't sure if it was the two years that had passed since I saw him or the fact that he was bigger than I remembered.

"So, I guess you belong to Maximum Capacity as well?" Peter asked.

"Um… yeah." I was having a hard time focusing on what he was saying. All I saw was his bare chest rippling with muscles. "Wait, what did you say?" I needed to get it together and act like an adult instead of an awestruck teenager.

"The gym, you must be a member too," Peter repeated himself, knowing perfectly well the effect he was having on me.

"Yeah, I just joined," I said, moving to the side so other members could pass.

Peter must have also sensed our conversation being interrupted by our choice of area. He gently grabbed my arm and pulled me down the hall near the men's locker room. "I think we're in the way."

Once we were out of the way, we continued our conversation. "You look good," Peter confessed, moving his hand from my arm and taking hold of my hand.

There was something different about him. It was almost as if he had regret in his eyes. When we parted ways, it wasn't the best break-up. We both said some things that shouldn't have been said. "You look good too."

I'm not sure what happened, whether it was the silence between us or the way we were looking at each other, but nothing could have prepared me for what happened next. Before I knew it, Peter lowered his lips to mine and kissed me. It wasn't your every day, glad-to-see-you kind of kiss. This kiss held so much more. When his tongue parted my lips, I knew I was in trouble. Something was igniting inside me that I couldn't control even if I tried. It was something that only Peter could make me feel.

We stared at each other for a moment, wondering what just happened. Whatever it was, there was something between us because before I could protest, Peter led me inside the men's locker room. Still holding tightly to my hand, he took me to one of the private bathrooms. I was pleasantly surprised when the scent of musk and spice mixed with sweat hit me, causing an electric bolt to surge through my body. Once we were inside the small room, Peter turned the lock on the door to make sure we wouldn't get caught.

Lifting my body and holding it against the door, he whispered as he gently kissed down my neck, "God, I missed you."

I wasn't sure how I felt at that moment. All I knew was I needed him. Being abstinent for two years wasn't something I had planned. I just never found anyone I was attracted to the way I was to Peter. With one hand clutching my ass, Peter slowly moved his other hand up my bare stomach and underneath my sports bra. Gliding his hand around my back, he was able to unclasp the hook in one swift movement. Removing my arms from around his shoulders, I took off my bra and dropped it to the floor. His hands were like magic on my body. I wasn't sure what it was about his touch that triggered something inside me.

Still holding me to the wall, Peter dipped his head and gently placed his mouth over my hard nipple. I could feel the wetness between my legs pool inside my thong panties. Peter set me down and carefully removed my yoga pants and panties, pushing them down my trembling legs. It had been too long. He hadn't even entered me, and I was shaking at the knees. While he was struggling to remove my bottoms, I was working to remove his shorts. Once we were both completely naked, he went to his knees and placed his mouth over my mound. A soft whimper escaped my mouth when his tongue swirled around my clit. "God, you're beautiful," he said, holding me at my waist as he continued to feast. Before I knew what happened, my body exploded with pleasure.

"I want to take you so badly, but I don't have a condom," he said regretfully.

Before I could let him know I was on the pill, there was a knock on the door. "Hey, are you okay in there?" A male voice sounded on the other side of the door.

As we looked at each other, trying not to laugh, Peter said, "I'm fine. Thanks for checking."

~****~

Peter and I managed to escape the confines of the small bathroom unnoticed. I wasn't sure what the gym's policy was on women entering the men's locker room, but neither of us was willing to find out. Why was there always that small moment after a sexual encounter that seemed to be so awkward? I didn't know what to say to Peter, even though there were so many things running through my head. Instead of taking a chance and saying something stupid, I headed to the women's locker room while Peter walked in the other direction. As if this moment couldn't get any more awkward, I was met again with a hard body. I needed to start watching where I was going.

"So, we meet again," the tall, handsome stranger announced as he took hold of my arms.

"Oh God, I'm so sorry," I replied, trying not to stare at his muscular chest. What was it about these men that made them unwilling to put a shirt on?

"You know, if we keep meeting like this, you're going to have to tell me your name," he said with a smile.

"Lilly, and you are?" I asked, feeling the heat radiating through my body.

"Pierre."

"Well, it's nice to meet you," I said, holding out my hand so that we could make the introduction official.

"As much as I'd rather chat more, I need to get to my handball match." He smiled. "It was nice meeting you, Lilly. Hopefully, we'll run into each other again."

"Good luck... with your match." I couldn't help but turn as he walked past me. I needed to make sure never to go two years without sex again. My libido was beginning to protest.

# CHAPTER SIX
## *Lilly*

Instead of taking my usual hot shower, I opted for a cold one. My body was overheating from the amount of testosterone I came in contact with within a short period of time. After taking a long shower, my body felt back to normal. I quickly slipped into the change of clothing I brought and headed out. Just as I was leaving, I heard Peter's voice behind me, calling my name. I was hoping to get away without running into him.

"Lilly, hold up," I heard him say as I stopped and waited for him to approach me. He must have showered as well, by the way, he looked. Even with wet hair, he was gorgeous. And the way he filled out his t-shirt was mouthwatering.

"Hey," I said.

"Can we go somewhere and talk?" he asked.

"Um... Sure." I wasn't sure what he had to talk about, but I was curious to find out.

I felt small against him as we began walking down the sidewalk. At some point during our walk, he took hold of my hand and brought it to his lips. Something was going on with him. When I looked up at him, I saw something in his eyes that I'd seen during our little episode in the locker room. There was compassion in them.

As we rounded the corner, my phone began to vibrate. I unzipped my bag and pulled it out. It was an unknown number, the same one that had been calling me for the past week. I had had enough of this caller. Without hesitation, I let whoever was calling have it. "Listen, you piece of shit. I don't know what you want, but quit calling me." When the phone went dead, I threw my phone back in my bag. "Asshole."

Peter stopped and looked over at me. "What the hell was that, Lilly?"

"Some asshole keeps calling me and doesn't say anything. Today was the last straw with him or her. I've had enough."

"How long has this been going on?" Peter asked in a commanding tone.

"I don't know. A week, maybe."

I could tell that Peter wasn't happy about the calls I was getting. I could see the change in his expression as it shifted from compassionate to tense. I think every vein in his neck was bulging out. As soon as we got to my condo, he asked me for my key. At first, I just looked at him, but then he began to snap his fingers like he was waiting for me to hand them over. Instead of fighting with him, I handed them over. I thought he was a little anal because of a stupid prank call. Leading the way inside, he made sure that I was behind him the whole time as he scanned the living room, then the other rooms—men and their alpha male egos.

"Satisfied?" I said, moving away from him to the kitchen.

He didn't say anything, but he knew what I was thinking. I thought only girls tended to roll their eyes. "Do you want a glass of wine or something stronger?" I asked.

"Do you have any beer?" he asked, making himself at home.

"Sure." Even though I wasn't typically a beer drinker, I kept a six-pack on hand in case I had any male guests.

I handed Peter his beer and sat in the chair across from him. I could have sat next to him, but the last thing I wanted was to give him the idea that I wanted him. I watched as the open end of the bottle touched his lips. I didn't realize what a turn on it was to watch him take a drink of beer from a bottle. The way his lip pressed against the lip of the bottle had me weak between the knees. Trying hard to compose myself, I took a sip of my wine and then asked nervously, "So what did you want to talk to me about?"

Setting his beer on the small table, he leaned forward and coiled his hands through his thick hair. I knew whatever he had to say was difficult for him. Even though I knew it was a big mistake, I got up and sat next to him and placed my arm around his broad shoulders. I could feel the tension in his body begin to relax.

"This is really hard for me, Lilly. I don't even know where to begin," he said, lifting his head and drawing his gaze to me.

There it was again, that look. I could have dived head first into those green eyes. "Just say it, Peter."

"Okay. Here it goes." He began rising to his feet. "You drive me crazy, Lilly. These past two years have been hell on me. You are all I think about. Even when I tried being with other women, you were the only person I thought about."

"Wait, you've been with other women?" I don't know why his admission surprised me. It wasn't like I expected him to wait for me, especially knowing how things between us ended.

"Damn, Lilly. What did you want me to do? You didn't give me any indication that you still wanted to be with me."

"That's because neither did you. You wouldn't tell me anything the day I left for Paris. If you had asked me to stay and not go, I wouldn't have left."

Peter was pacing back and forth in my small living room. I thought for sure he was going to wear my shaggy rug to mere fibers. When he stopped and turned towards me, my heart sank into my stomach. I wished I knew what he was thinking. He soon let me know. He took me by my hands and forced me to stand so that we were face to face. Lifting his hands to my face, he gently cupped my cheeks. "I want us to try again, Lilly. I want things back the way they were before you left for Paris."

The way he looked at me confused me more than ever. I didn't know if this was something that I wanted. I didn't want to go through the same pain I had two years ago. I knew I was the one who left, but he made it clear that he wanted us to go our separate ways. He was unwilling to make it work. I felt there was something more than me just leaving. He was hiding something.

Before I could say anything, my cell phone began ringing. Stepping away from Peter, I found my bag and pulled out my phone. It was Natalie. "Hey, Natalie," I greeted her, hoping she wouldn't hear the tension in my voice.

"I couldn't wait to call you. I have good news. The seller accepted your offer. It looks like you have a new home for your gallery," she said excitedly.

"That's wonderful. When am I going to be able to start moving in?" I answered, unable to contain my eagerness.

"Well, since it's a cash deal, we can close in a couple of days. I just need to get the proper documents together. I'll let you know the exact date."

"The sooner, the better, Natalie. Thanks for everything."

Placing my phone on the counter, I turned back to Peter, who was sitting on the couch sipping his beer. Walking towards him, I took his half-empty beer bottle and set it on the coffee table. Looking at him, confused, I said, "This is all too sudden. I needed a little time to think about things."

Peter placed his hand on my cheek and pulled me close to him. Our lips met without hesitation. My lips parted, wanting to feel his warmth inside. I could feel his softness as he began intertwining his tongue with mine. The warmth of his breath on me filled my senses with comfort. As the kiss deepened even more, he began moving his hands down my body until they rested on my hips. In one swift movement, he lifted my body onto his so that I was straddling his muscular legs. I didn't know how much I wanted him. I just knew I couldn't stop how he was making me feel. No matter what happened between us in the past, at this moment, all I wanted was him.

Taking hold of the bottom of his t-shirt, I pulled it up over his head. His chest came into view, which made me desire him even more. I broke our kiss and lowered my head, placing kiss after kiss down his neck to his chest, where I placed my mouth over his hardened nipple. Swirling my tongue around the hard peak, I began lightly sucking and kissing. I heard a low moan escape his mouth as I moved over to the other side and gave his other nipple the same attention. Before I could finish my assault, Peter had me up in the air and on my back. As his large body leaned over me, I watched his muscles contract as he held himself above me.

"Are you sure this is what you want? Because I won't be able to stop once I start," Peter whispered softly as he nibbled my ear lobe.

"Yes, I want this. I want you." I couldn't and didn't want him to stop. My body was on fire and in need of release. All I could think about was having him buried deep inside me.

Peter slowly removed my shirt and quickly unfastened the front clasp of my lacy bra. All I wanted was his hands on my body. I needed to feel him touch me. When he took hold of my taut nipple, I was more than ready for more. Pulling his body closer to mine, I forked my fingers through his thick hair and pulled his mouth to mine. When our lips met, I was consumed by his scent. All I could think about was how much I needed him. As our tongues lapped together, Peter began working on the zipper of my jeans. It was taking too long for him to get them undone and off me. Lifting my hips, I lowered my hands and helped him pull my pants down over my hips. His hand slowly worked at removing my underwear while I worked at getting the rest of his clothing off.

It took some effort since we were unwilling to separate, but we were finally naked, bare skin to bare skin. Peter looked down at me with those green eyes and a small smile splayed across his face. As he kissed his way down my body, I could feel the heat begin to erupt. My body was on fire and needed to be bathed in pure pleasure. Peter's soft kisses reached the apex of my mound, sending my body soaring. Despite his slow movements, I could feel the sensation his magic tongue was doing on my clit. I was ready to combust. His tongue seeped lower between my slick folds, causing my back to arch off the couch. It was when he plunged, not one but two fingers inside me, that I came undone. My desire took over and spilled with fury. It was then that I knew there was no way I could be without this man. He may have had my body, but not my heart. My release calmed, and Peter pulled his body from mine. Even though he had satisfied my hunger, I still wanted more. I needed to feel him inside me. Tugging his hard body back to me, I could see a smile brighten his face

"Hold on, baby," he said as he proceeded to push from me.

I watched as he lifted his pants from the floor and pulled out a condom from his wallet. It was then that I knew he needed more too. When he straddled my hips, I stared down at his impressive erection and watched as he rolled on the condom. He leaned over and gave me a tender kiss. "Are you ready, baby?" he asked softly.

"Yes, I need you inside me."

Taking hold of his cock with one hand while propping his body over me with the other, he positioned his cock at my entrance and began slowly moving inside me. I wasn't sure if it was his size or the fact that I hadn't been with any man for two years that caused a little pain as he drove inside. "God, baby, you're so tight. Are you okay?" he breathed, taking it slow.

I tried to hold back the pain I was feeling. I didn't want him to stop. "I'm good, don't stop."

The more he moved inside me, the more I could take of him. Every movement inside brought me closer to release. God, he felt so good. I could feel that I was getting close to my release. Peter took hold of my arms and placed them above my head. As he continued to thrust deeper inside, he commanded. "Don't come until I tell you."

I wasn't sure how much longer I could wait. I was so close; it took everything I had to hold back my release. When I was almost at my breaking point, he finally commanded, "Come, baby, I'm right there."

My body shook with intense pleasure; I thought I was going to pass out. Peter must have felt my body give way because he emptied inside me with one final thrust. "God, I missed you," he breathed softly.

~****~

It was late by the time Peter left my condo. We ended up sharing some Chinese takeout and watching a movie. We really didn't talk too much about what went on in our lives over the past two years, mostly because I was afraid to hear about all the women he had been with. Even though I didn't expect him to give up a social life, I couldn't bring myself to think about him ever being with someone else.

After we said our goodbyes, he suggested that one of his men kept an eye on my condo, just to be safe. It was either that or letting him spend the night. I thought it was a little over the top since it was only pranked calls and nothing more. I didn't think to mention the incident with Mrs.

Jensen's cat. I wasn't one-hundred percent sure that I forgot to lock my door. It only made sense since nothing was disturbed or taken.

For the first time in forever, I was finally able to sleep soundly. Even though I still had dreams about Peter, at least I woke up with an ending to them. I also felt refreshed and energized, which I hadn't felt for a long time. Pushing from my bed, I headed to the bathroom to take a shower and begin my day. I wanted to get in touch with Natalie to see if I could get another look at the building. I wanted to get a better idea of how I wanted the area to be laid out. I knew I wanted to change the lighting and close off space for an office and a conference room. I also wanted to have the area separated into different sections to showcase each artist's work. With two floors to work with, I had enough room to display various kinds of art, ranging from abstract to still life. I also needed to come up with a name for the gallery. I spent all morning trying to decide on what to name it. I wanted the name to reflect the kind of art that would be displayed and still have a catchy name that would be remembered. After careful consideration, I decided to name the new gallery 'Séduire,' which is French for Allure. I thought it would be a perfect name, considering I intended to get as many people as possible to step inside the gallery.

Natalie was kind enough to meet me at the new location. Once inside, I pulled out my notepad and began drawing out how I wanted the galley to be laid out. I was like an artist working with a blank canvas. Even though it was only a rough draft, I thought it looked pretty good. Now, it was a matter of getting a contractor to do the work. I trusted only one contractor, so I called him and let him know what I wanted. We decide to meet later in the week to go over the details and then lay out a plan to start. I was glad when he told me that his schedule was open and his next big project wouldn't be until next month.

# CHAPTER SEVEN
## *Lilly*

When I got back to my apartment, I was surprised to see an unfamiliar, but good-looking alpha-male type standing outside my door. I could only wonder who he was. I fumbled with my purse to find my keys, ensuring that my pepper spray was within reach. Walking up to the guy, I looked at him with curiosity and politely asked, "Can I help you with something?"

He didn't even make eye contact with me when he said, "No, ma'am."

It wasn't the answer I wanted, so I questioned him further. "Okay, do you mind telling me why you're standing by my front door?"

This time he made eye contact. "Just following orders, ma'am."

This conversation was going nowhere. "Look, I don't know who the fuck you are, but if you don't move away from my door, I'm going to call the police." Instead of reaching for the pepper spray, I pulled out my phone, ready to dial 9-1-1.

"No need for that, ma'am. I work for Jagged Edge Security. I have orders to make sure nothing happens to you," he said in a stern voice.

"Did Peter put you up to this?" I could feel the blood begin to boil in my body. How could he possibly think that he could just step in and order protection for me? This was so unbelievable, I couldn't even think straight. It was one thing to have someone watch my building, but to have them stand guard outside my door was another. What would the neighbors think?

"Yes, ma'am. My name is Cop."

The big guy named 'Cop' moved aside and allowed me to enter my apartment. Placing my things on the counter, except for my cell, I brought Peter's number up. By the time I finished with him, he was going to wish he never sent one of his guys to take up residence at my door.

I waited in my kitchen, thumping my fingers against the countertop until Peter answered his phone. When the call went to voice mail, all I could do was leave a message. "Peter, are you frickin' crazy? I want this guy standing in front of my door gone! Do you understand? Gone!"

I hung up and went to the fridge to pull out a bottle of wine. I was steaming and needed something to cool me off. I poured the wine into a glass and took a big drink. By the time I had finished the second glass of wine, I was feeling a lot calmer. Even though I was still pissed, at least my body was no longer boiling over. I walked over to the peephole in the door and saw that 'Cop' was still standing outside. I needed to stay away from the door; it only made me angrier the more I thought about it. Taking my glass of wine and the bottle, I went to the bathroom to take a bath. Whenever I got angry or upset, this was the only thing that could calm my anger. A long bath and wine, a perfect combination.

My body wasn't only warm, but numb. Polishing off a whole bottle of wine while in the tub probably wasn't one of my better ideas. Listening to my iPod playing loudly not only blocked out my thoughts, but it also blocked out the pounding taking place on my bathroom door. It was only when I looked up that I saw a man fit to be tied. He was pissed.

"What the fuck, Lilly!" I pulled the earbuds from my ears only to catch the last part of his yelling.

"What are you doing here? And why did you just bust down my bathroom door?" I asked sharply, as I was beginning to sober up.

"When you didn't answer your phone, I got worried. Cop knocked on your door, but you wouldn't answer. Do you have any idea how angry I am right now?" As Peter walked closer to me, I was becoming more and more aware of his anger. I was also beginning to feel a little uncomfortable, considering he was fully clothed, and the diminishing bubbles barely covered me.

Wrapping my earbuds around my iPod and placing it on the edge of the tub, I calmly said, "Can you stop yelling and please hand me a towel?"

Peter grabbed the towel I laid on the counter. There was something in the way he was looking at me that caused my heart to beat faster. It was no longer a look of anger, but one of desire. The last thing I wanted was to end up having sex with him. I was still furious. As I wrapped the towel around my body, I slowly tried to get out of the tub. Needless to say, it wasn't an easy task. I must have lost my footing because I fell right into his arms as I was beginning to climb out. Peter grabbed me around my waist and held me close to his body. Being so close to him, I could smell musk and spice. That was all it took, I was hooked. I placed my head against his chest and breathed in his scent.

Peter lifted me in his arms and carried me to my bed. Everything I felt moments ago was gone. I was no longer angry with him. All I wanted was to be near him. Lying on the bed, I watched as he began opening my drawers, pulling out a pair of lacy panties and a t-shirt. God, he looked good standing in front of me. "Do you need help getting these on, or can you do it yourself?" he asked in a stern voice.

Sitting up, I took the items from him and pushed myself from the bed. My towel fell to the floor as I began swaying. I sat back on the edge of the bed and started getting dressed. I could feel Peter watching every move I made. I knew he was getting turned on more than I already was. Standing up, I took his hand and placed it on my breast. I don't know what caused me to be so bold. Maybe it was the wine, or maybe it was just the desire I had for this man.

Peter moved his hand from my breast and wrapped it around my waist. Pulling me closer to his body, he placed his lips on mine and gently kissed me. The minute his tongue entered my mouth, I was lost. I wanted him more than any man I had ever wanted. Peter lifted me from the floor and gently placed me on the bed. Just when I thought he would have me, he pulled his body from mine and pulled the covers over me.

"Don't you want me?" I asked with confusion.

"More than you will ever know, Lilly. But I can't take you the way you are." Peter leaned over and gave me a tender kiss on my forehead. "Go to sleep, and we'll talk in the morning."

"Can you at least stay with me?"

"I can do that," he replied as he slowly crawled into bed beside me, still fully clothed.

As much as I wanted him, I settled for him being next to me. So when he pulled me to his side and wrapped his arms around me, I was content. Being next to the warmth of his body was all I needed. Within minutes my eyes closed, and I entered a blissful sleep.

~****~

Waking up in the morning, my head was pounding. I knew I shouldn't have drunk all that wine. As I rolled over, I felt an empty space beside me. I wasn't too drunk to remember that Peter had slept with me. I tried to keep my eyes open, but the sun was shining through the blinds, causing even more pain to my throbbing head. Pulling on the blind cord, I adjusted the amount of sunlight coming through. Rolling on my other side, I noticed a small note and two ibuprofen tablets, along with a full glass of water, sitting on the nightstand. Picking up the note, I read the words, *'Take these and drink the full glass of water'* in very neat handwriting. I took the two tablets in my hand and popped them into my mouth. When I had the full glass of water down, I rolled back over on my back and closed my eyes.

I wasn't sure what time it was, but my phone was going off like crazy. Lifting my body from my bed, I headed into the kitchen to retrieve my phone and turn off the annoying sound. It was only then that I noticed that a pot of coffee had already been made. Leaning up against a lone coffee mug on the counter was another note. As shitty as I felt, I couldn't help but smile. Walking to the coffee mug, I picked up the note. This one was a little longer.

*I can only imagine how you're feeling this morning. I have boiled you some eggs, and there is fresh fruit in the fridge. I'm guessing that you have slept most of the morning, but we need to talk. Call me as soon as you are done eating and have showered.*

*Peter*

Rolling my eyes at the note, I opened the fridge and took out the two hard-boiled eggs and the small bowl of fruit. Next, I poured myself a mug full of coffee and added my favorite creamer. As I was sitting at the bar, I wondered why I was drinking last night in the first place. Walking over to the front door, I looked through the peephole. "Yep, still there," I said out loud as I walked back to the kitchen. One thing was certain: Peter and I were definitely going to talk.

Just as I was finishing getting dressed, there was a knock at my door. I thought it was kind of strange considering I had a 6'5" alpha-male standing outside my door. Taking a quick look at myself in the mirror, I decided even though I wasn't a hundred percent, I looked pretty good. When I pulled the door open, I was surprised to see Peter standing next to Cop. Usually, it would have been a woman's dream to see two gorgeous, hunky men standing in front of her, but for me, it was only annoying.

Stepping aside, I watched as Peter entered my condo. God, he looked good, I thought to myself. Shutting the door, I turned to face him. "I thought you wanted me to call you when I was ready."

"Couldn't wait any longer," he said, taking a seat on the couch.

I took my spot on the chair beside him. We sat for what seemed like an eternity in silence. I couldn't stand it anymore, so I just came out with it. "I think maybe we need to rethink this thing with us."

Looking up at me, he let out a chuckle. "Really, because I don't think you were rethinking anything last night.

Matter of fact, it looked to me like you wanted to fuck me any way you could."

"Last night was a mistake." I needed to get it together. I needed to put my feelings for this man behind me and focus on the real reason we could never be together.

"Umm, I see. So, this is how it's going to be, just like two years ago," Peter said.

"What happened two years ago has nothing to do with this. It's your controlling behavior. You think you can do whatever you want, whenever you want, without any regard to how I feel."

"If this is about Cop, I'm not going to apologize for having him outside your door. For God's sake, Lilly, don't you get it? Don't you think it's a little odd that you come back to New York, and all of a sudden, you start getting strange calls?"

"I can take care of myself, Peter. I want him gone." I wasn't about to give in to him. Besides, I hadn't received a call in two days. Whomever it was probably figured out that they had the wrong number.

Standing, Peter walked over to where I was sitting. Taking me by the hands, he pulled me to a standing position. He was at least seven inches taller than me, so when he lifted my chin to meet his eyes, I could do nothing to resist. Capturing my mouth with his, he gently parted my lips and dove in for the kill. He had me. I was like putty in his hands. Breaking the kiss, he looked down at me and whispered, "I care about you, Lilly. Please let me keep you safe."

There was nothing I could do except agree with him. He kissed my forehead and began walking away. "Wait, where are you going?" I asked, needing a little bit more of what he just gave me.

"I need to take care of a few things. I'll be back around 7:00 p.m. Be ready." With that, he opened the door and left me standing there, once again hot and unfulfilled.

This guy was so infuriating. Things haven't changed with him. Closing the door and grunting with irritation, I looked at the time. It was only 1:00 p.m. I still had plenty of time to get ready for whatever he had in store for me. Walking to the kitchen, I poured myself a much-needed cup of coffee. Grabbing my laptop, I perched myself on my couch and began pulling up all my resources. I was thankful that I had found a reliable contractor, so the only thing left to do was to find an assistant and a maintenance man. Just as my laptop came to life, I heard some talking in the hallway. I could hear two people arguing. My curiosity got the best of me as I walked to the door and looked out the peephole. Unfortunately, I couldn't see much. I did, however, notice that Cop was no longer standing in front of my door. Cracking my door as quietly as I could, I tried to listen to the conversation.

"You aren't supposed to be here, Sean. You're breaking the restraining order I have on you," the woman barked.

"I just need you to listen, Brie. I'm sorry. I should never have hit you," he confessed.

"Yeah, well, you did, and now it's over, and you have to leave," she stated.

"I'm never going to let you go, Brie. When I come back, I'm going to make things right," The man, dressed in military fatigues, turned and walked away.

When I saw that the coast was clear, I opened my door and walked up to the woman. As I watched her gather her belongings that must have fallen to the floor during their altercation, I couldn't help but walk over and help her. "Hey, are you okay?" I asked, bending down to help her with her things.

"Yeah, thanks," she said, smiling.

"I'm Lilly, by the way. I live across the hall."

"I'm Sabrina, but everyone calls me Brie," she said.

"Well, it's nice to meet you. Did you just move in? I've lived here for some time and never noticed you before."

"Yeah, I moved in a couple of days ago. I don't know how long I'll be here, though. I recently got laid off from the law firm I worked at, and working at a coffee shop doesn't exactly pay the bills." Brie said regretfully.

"I might be able to help you out. I'm opening a new art gallery and looking for a good assistant."

"Thanks for the offer, but I don't know anything about art," Brie confessed, stuffing the rest of her things in her bag.

"I'll teach you. Besides, it will save me the time of interviewing." Even though I just met Brie, I could tell she wanted a better job. Even though Dylan was my best friend, it would be nice to have another female friend.

# CHAPTER EIGHT
## *Lilly*

Peter was right on time. I wasn't sure what he had planned, so I chose to wear something simple: a pair of skinny jeans and a pink lacy tank top. Taking a last look at myself in the mirror, I went to answer the door. There in front of me stood a man that oozed male domination. He was wearing faded jeans, a black v-neck t-shirt, and a leather jacket. I could feel a tingle between my legs, letting me know the effect this man had on me. Still staring at his gorgeousness, I somehow manage to step aside so that he could come through the door. He gently swiped his thumb across my lips, which set my body on fire. I could feel my nipples harden beneath my lacy tank. Trying hard not to show the effect he was having on me, I closed the door and said, "So where are we going?"

Looking down at my five-inch peep-toe stilettos, he said, "You may want to change your shoes. I brought my bike."

"Oh," I said, surprised, looking down at my feet and my pink toenails peeking out. "I didn't know you had a motorcycle."

"There are a lot of things you don't know about me, Lilly," he advised. "You may want to grab a jacket too. It could get chilly."

Leaving the condo after I changed into my boots and gray leather jacket, we headed out into the night. The sun was just setting, but it was still pretty warm. Parked in front of my building was a sleek black Harley with shiny chrome tailpipes on each side. I had never seen anything more beautiful. Handing me a helmet, Peter straddled the bike and started the engine. I just stood there and watched as his thigh muscles flexed tightly against his jeans. Taking my hand, he helped me get on the bike. I had never ridden one, so I wasn't sure where to hold him. He must have felt my concern because he took first one hand, then the other, and wrapped them around his waist. "Hold on tight, baby," he said as we began moving away from the curb.

Even though I had a helmet on, I could feel the warm air blowing against my face. I began to appreciate the reason behind owning a motorcycle. It gave me a feeling of freedom. I didn't know what it was, but I felt safe holding on to Peter. Not because I would probably fall off if I didn't, but because I knew he wouldn't let anything happen to me. Sitting behind him, I placed my head against his shoulder and took in his scent. With the wind blowing, his scent was even more addictive than before.

Moments later, we were out of the city on our way through the Holland Tunnel and into New Jersey. I wasn't sure where we were going, but I was enjoying the ride nonetheless.

As we turned onto Morgan Street, a beautiful building came into view. It was lit up with bright lights and must have been at least fifty floors high. As Peter entered the parking garage, I could only assume that he lived here, or at least someone he knew did. Working his way through the garage, he finally pulled into a spot next to a black Camaro. I remembered him owning one, so once again, I assumed it was his.

Peter helped me remove my helmet and steadied me as I got off the bike. My legs were a little wobbly from the ride. I tried not to think about how the vibration of the engine mixed with being so close to Peter may have been the cause. Taking my hand, Peter led me to the elevators. Once inside, I watched as the passing floors began to light up on the display. We finally stopped at the twenty-ninth floor.

As I followed behind him, I took in the decor. The hall was decorated with beige and tan walls, and the carpeting had a swirl design of various shades of browns, tans, and oranges. Peter stopped in front of a door that held the number 2912 in gold plating.

When I stepped inside, it was nothing like what I had expected. The floor transitioned from tile to wood. As I looked to my left, there was a good-sized kitchen area that had light-colored cabinets, granite countertops, and a small breakfast bar. As we walked further in, we entered what I presumed was the living area. It was also a good size. It was decorated in gray and white. A small dining set that sat six opened up to a living room furnished with a cream-colored couch and two gray matching armchairs. One wall featured floor-to-ceiling windows, which showed a magnificent view of Manhattan across the Hudson River.

As I continued to take in my surroundings, I couldn't help but ask, "Do you live here?"

I could feel Peter coming up behind me. His breath was warm on my head as he said, "Yes, Lilly, this is where I live. You seem a little surprised."

"I am actually. This is not what I was expecting. I guess a lot has changed in two years." The last time I was at Pete's place, he lived in a one-bedroom apartment with barely enough room to turn around in.

Peter grabbed my arm and spun me around to face him. "Come on. Let me show the rest of the place."

After Peter showed me the rest of his home, which consisted of two bedrooms also decorated in gray and white, two full bathrooms, and one game room, we headed back to the kitchen area, where he poured me a glass of wine.

Taking places on his couch, he mentioned casually, "I thought we could eat in. I ordered Italian ahead of time. I hope that's okay?"

"That's fine. I'm starving," I confessed as I set my wine glass on the glass coffee table while I slipped off my jacket. I wasn't sure if it was the warmth I felt between my legs or the effect the wine was having on me.

Just as I was about to grab my glass of wine, Peter took hold of my hand and brought it to his lips. I could feel the softness of his lips as his mouth touched my skin. All I could do was stare at the contact his mouth made with the back of my hand. I could feel the warmth between my legs turn into an inferno. When the doorbell rang, I took a sigh of relief as Peter stood to answer it. "That must be our dinner."

As quickly as he left the room, I had the full contents of my wine down my throat. Fanning my face, I tried to keep my feelings for this man at bay. I could hear Peter talking to the delivery guy from where I was sitting. It was my cue to assist him with dinner. Taking my empty glass and his full one, I walked over to the dining room table and placed his glass on the smooth surface. Spotting the bottle of wine, I stepped to the bar and poured myself another drink. Peter was already in the kitchen, getting our plates ready. There were two servings of chicken Marsala, garlic bread, and Caesar salad. I wasn't sure where he ordered the food from, but it smelled delicious.

An hour later, we were back on the couch, completely stuffed from the wonderful meal. The silence between us suddenly became very awkward. It felt like being on a first date and waiting for someone to say something or make the first move. Staring across the room at the black TV screen, I heard Peter's words. "Lilly, there's something I need to ask you."

Turning my body so it was angled towards his, I replied hesitantly, "Shoot."

"Do you know of anybody that would be calling you and then hanging up?" he asked, looking at me with concern.

"How would I know, Peter? Not too many people have my number, and the people that do would never call and hang up on me without saying anything." I wasn't sure where Peter was going with this, but everyone I knew had no reason to do this.

"I just thought it might have been one of your boyfriends you saw back in Paris," Peter said.

"Are you kidding me?" I said as I start to stand. "I haven't been with anyone, Peter. I think it's time that I left."

Picking up my jacket, I slipped it on and grabbed my small purse.

"Wait, Lilly," I heard him say as I got to the door. "Don't leave."

Just as I turned my body to tell him where he could stick it, his lips were on mine. I couldn't resist the touch of his mouth over mine. My body began melting into his as his tongue parted my lips and began massaging mine. Our bodies were pressed together as I wrapped my hands around his shoulders. I felt like I couldn't get close enough to him. With our lips still pressed together, Peter began walking us back into the living area while removing my jacket. My hands left his body, trying to assist him any way I could to get it off. The jacket fell to the floor with a thud, and once again, my arms found their way back around his shoulders. Peter's hands moved down my back, resting on my cheeks. Before I knew it, I wrapped my legs around his waist as Peter lifted me from the floor and began heading down a short hallway, where I assumed his bedroom was.

Peter gently placed my body on the bed while leaning over me, careful not to crush me. Both of us were frantically trying to get each other's clothing off. Tugging at his t-shirt, I finally got it off his hard body. He began wildly removing my top. I could feel his heart beating as he dipped down and kissed me on the lips. The taste of wine on his tongue and the scent of musk on his skin had me wanting more. Lowering my hands, I tried desperately to undo his jeans. There was no room between us, so I rolled over, taking him with me. With my body straddling him, I broke our kiss and began undoing the button on his jeans, freeing him from the confines. He helped me push his jeans and boxers down his muscular legs, making his cock spring to full attention. I looked up at him and licked my lips before placing small shallow kisses down his hard body. His moans of pleasure let me know that he wanted me as much as I wanted him, if not more.

Taking hold of his shaft, I began caressing it with my hand like a well-played instrument. The smooth, soft skin glided through my fingers as a drop of pre-cum began to form at the tip. Lowering my head, I swirled my tongue over the head and lapped up his creamy essence. Stroking him with my hand, I took what I could of him in my mouth. His hips began moving with me as I tried to take more of him. I heard another moan escape his lips, letting me know that he was enjoying my assault on his penis.

"God, I love your mouth, baby," he groaned as his hips begin pumping harder, pushing his cock deeper inside my mouth.

Licking and sucking him, I could feel that he was close. I opened for him further, allowing his cock to hit the back of my throat. I could feel him growing as his release began to fill his shaft. Without warning, he lifted me from his cock and gently placed me back on the bed. "I need to be inside you, baby," he said, his eyes focused on mine.

Peter quickly unfastened the button on my jeans and began lowering them down my legs. I could feel his breath on me as he placed his mouth at my cleft. I was going crazy with need. As I opened wider for him, he pulled at my lacy thong and ripped it away. My heart began to pound faster, anticipating his next move. When his mouth swirled around my clit, I just about lost it. I had been sex-deprived for so long that even the slightest touch had me soaring. Peter slid his finger down my slick folds and entered me while his tongue was doing magical things to my clit. I could feel the pressure in my stomach tighten as he curled his finger to caress my g-spot. I couldn't hold on any longer. My orgasm consumed me as my legs began to shake, and my body shuddered with pure ecstasy.

Peter slowly pulled from me, making his way up my sensitized body. He positioned his knees between my legs, opening me wider. Lunging forward, he slowly entered me while my body tried to take him. I could feel my entrance stretch as I took him inch by pleasurable inch. My sex began to pulsate with every thrust of his cock. Lowering his head, he took hold of my nipple between his teeth, just enough to cause a jet of electricity to reach my core. My body couldn't take anymore, and it gave way to pure satisfaction. I could feel his release when his cock spasmed, and his body started to tighten with uncontrollable pleasure.

# CHAPTER NINE
## *Lilly*

Leaving Peter's the night before last left me wondering if being with him was such a good idea. I knew the more I gave in to him, the harder it would be for me to break things off. The only problem was that I wasn't sure if that was what I wanted. My heart told me that I wanted more than anything to be with him, but my head kept saying to let him go. Needing to focus on something other than Peter, I remembered that tonight was Tetralogy Innovations' grand opening. I was so happy for Dylan. It had taken her a long time to get where she was, with the unexpected complication with the construction of the new building, but her day was finally here. I, on the other hand, still had so much to do before having my own opening. In less than two hours, I would be the proud owner of my very own gallery, something that I had always dreamed of. And the nice thing about it was that I did it by myself. With the money I had saved and the money my parents put aside for me in a trust fund, I was finally able to break free and earn my own living.

Being on my way to my success meant I needed to get a move on if I was going to meet Natalie in time to sign the paperwork transferring ownership. Sliding from my bed, I stripped away my pajamas and headed to the shower. But before I did, I looked out the window to see if the day looked as wonderful as I felt. Taking a quick peek through my bedroom blinds, I could see that the sun was shining, and the heat from the sun's rays had already warmed the pane of the window.

Forty-five minutes later, I was showered, dressed, and ready for the day. Natalie thought it would be nice to meet at the gallery since it was the center place for everyone. She made special arrangements for the title company to present the documents. I was just getting out of the taxi when I noticed someone who looked familiar walking into the small café across the street. It was Sabrina.

"Brie," I yelled as I proceeded to cross the street.

"Hey," she said, meeting me as I stepped onto the curb.

"So, is this where you work?" I asked, glancing at her attire and noticing her pink apron with a cow holding a cup of coffee in his hoof.

"Yep," she said, hold the hem of her apron up with a smile. "Creamy and delicious. No artificial flavoring."

"I'll have to remember that," I said, looking across the street, noticing that Natalie was unlocking the door. "Listen, I need to go. I'm closing on the new gallery today. I'll stop by later, if that's okay?"

"Sounds good," Brie said, smiling back.

Just as I crossed the street, Natalie entered the building. She must not have noticed me talking to Brie from across the street. When I got to the door, it was still open, so I just headed inside. There was already a table with refreshments along with a table with several chairs set up. Hearing my heels on the wooden floor, Natalie turned my way.

"Hey, Lilly, how are you? Are you ready to get this done with?" Natalie asked.

"More than ready. Mostly I can't wait to start remodeling this place," I answered.

The current owner of the building walked through the door. He was an older gentleman with graying hair. He wasn't bad looking, but he definitely had one too many donuts.

"Mr. Tanner, how are you?" Natalie asked as she walked towards him with her hand extended.

"Very well, thank you," the older gentleman said.

"I'd like you to meet Lilly Davis. She is the buyer of your property," Natalie explained.

Walking up to him, I held out my hand. "It's so nice to meet you, Mr. Tanner. This is a lovely building."

"Please, please call me Bill," he said.

It took a little over an hour for us to finish signing the documents. I was now the proud owner of what was going to be Séduire Art Gallery. I couldn't wait to get started. The contractor was going to meet me here in about an hour, and since I had some time to spare, I thought this would be the perfect time to go across the street to where Brie worked. Having the shiny new keys in my hand, I locked up the gallery and walked over to the Happy Cow Coffee Shop. Someone must have been on drugs when they came up with that name, I thought to myself.

As I entered the small shop, I was pleasantly surprised to see that it was a really nice coffee place. Inside were bar-height tables butted up against the front windows, with some regular tables along the sides. In the middle were armchairs of various colors, along with round tables separating them. It was really very inviting. Some of the patrons took advantage of the comfortable armchairs while they worked on their laptop computers. I didn't see Brie right away when I walked in, so I went to the counter and asked if she was available.

Brie showed up a few minutes later and said she could take her break. I went ahead and ordered a pumpkin spice latte and grabbed one of the high tables against the window. I could see myself coming here often to grab a cup of coffee.

I must have been daydreaming because I didn't hear Brie coming up behind me. Tapping my shoulder lightly, she asked, "So what do you think?"

"I really like this place. It isn't at all what I expected," I confessed.

"Yeah, I hear that a lot," Brie confirmed, taking a seat across from me.

"So, have you thought about being my new assistant?" I asked, sipping my coffee.

"Kind of, but I would really like to stay working here. Would you consider letting me work for you part-time? Just to see if it is something I might want to do full-time," Brie asked.

"Of course," I said.

We were talking non-stop, and I didn't realize the time. "Oh shit, I've got to go. Can I catch up with you tomorrow?" I asked.

"You bet. I get off at six."

"Great, see you then."

After meeting with the contractor and showing him what I wanted for the gallery, I was utterly exhausted. By the time I got to my condo, my feet felt like they were ready for a three-week holiday. As I entered my condo, all I wanted was to soak in the tub. I had a least a few hours before Dylan's opening to get lost in lots and lots of bubbles.

Once I was in the tub, and the warmth of the water engulfed me, my body began to sing. The ache in my body started to go away, and I felt more relaxed. As much as I didn't want to disappoint my best friend, I could have just stayed the way I was at that very moment, but I knew this was an important night for her and I wouldn't hear the end of it if I didn't attend.

# CHAPTER TEN
## *Lilly*

Rade had sent a car for me, which I thought was very nice, considering the amount of alcohol I was planning on consuming. It was no surprise that Richard would be my driver. When I walked out of my building, he was already waiting for me by the back passenger door. He opened the door and said, "Good evening, Ms. Davis."

"Richard, please call me Lilly," I said as I got into the town car.

As we were driving, all I could think about was Peter. We hadn't seen each other for a couple of days. He said that he would be busy and would get with me as soon as he had a free moment. I couldn't understand what was so important that he couldn't call or text me. I hated the fact that I was now having the same feelings as before. I just couldn't be with someone who had so many secrets and was continually hiding things from me.

Half an hour later, we arrived at our destination. Dylan really went all-out for the event. She even had valet parking for all of the guests. Richard dropped me off in front of the massive building. It was actually a beautiful building. When Rade had purchased the place, he wanted to tear it down and start over, but Dylan talked him out of it. Instead, they ended up remodeling the outside and adding a different entrance. I would have to say that I'm glad they did. The curved archway with the steel beams made the building look futuristic. Even the dark windows down the entire length of the building gave it an ultra-modern look.

Making my way inside, I could hear the chattering of the crowd. I could tell the event was in full swing, making it a complete success for Dylan. It made my heart sing to know that so many people wanted to be a part of this for her. As I went further into the building, I could see several waiters with trays of champagne walking about. I waited patiently until one was within arm's reach before I snatched one of the crystal flutes from his tray. Holding on to his arm, I downed the bubbly liquid and grabbed another.

I began scanning the room to see if I could find Dylan. I spotted her immediately. It wasn't that hard, considering she was the only pregnant woman in the room. She was also the only woman that had a glow about her like an angel. Proceeding to walk towards her, I felt a light tug on my arm. When I turned around, I saw that it was Peter who had a hold of me. He was the last person I expected to see here. As far as I knew, he was away on business. At least that was how he made it sound when I last spoke to him.

"What are you doing here, Peter? I thought you were away on business," I said coldly.

"I was, and now I'm back," he said matter-of-factly.

"Well, if you'll excuse me, I need to say hello to Dylan," I said, pulling away from his grasp.

I could only guess what Peter was thinking, despite the look on his face. I was pretty sure he didn't see anything wrong with his behavior over the past few days. I felt it was only right to let him feel what I was feeling: rejected. When I finally got to Dylan after making it through the large crowd, she was talking with Evan. Evan was Rade's half-brother. I guess his father had an affair with his mother while still married. Dylan didn't tell me all the sordid details, but I knew Evan and Rade had become very close in the last couple of years. It made me wish that I had a brother or sister.

I gently tapped on Dylan's shoulder, watching her face light up when she looked at me. Hugging me, I smiled at Evan as he watched us. "This place is amazing, Dylan. There are so many people here," I said, pulling from her embrace.

"I know. Isn't it crazy? I never expected so many people to show up," Dylan stated.

As we carried on our conversation about the opening and then about my new gallery, I could feel someone's eyes upon me. Peter was watching my every move. It felt like he was a lion, and I was his prey, the way his eyes were fixed on me. No longer able to stand it, I excused myself and walked right up to him. "What is your problem?" I questioned him.

"What is your problem, Lilly? Ever since I got here, you've been as cold as ice." Peter forcefully whispered as he lowered his head to my ear.

"What's the matter, Peter? Can't take your own medicine?"

"This is not the place to have this discussion." Peter took hold of my arm and began leading me out of the room.

"Where are you taking me?" I asked.

"Somewhere, we won't be heard."

I wasn't sure where we were going, but it seemed as though Peter knew his way around the building. It didn't surprise me, especially since his company handled all of the security for Rade. Somehow we ended up on the elevator and ascending to the second floor. Peter directed me into one of the offices and closed the door, making sure to lock it.

"What is this about, Peter? I'm not sure what you have to say, but I'm tired of your dancing around everything. This is why it will never work between us. There are too many secrets," I said before he could stop me.

"There was something I needed to take care of," he admitted.

"Like what, Peter?"

"Something from my past."

"What was it, Peter?"

"Something that has nothing to do with us, or the way I feel about you," Peter said as he walked closer to me.

I backed away from him, needing to keep my distance. His explanation of where he went was still not good enough for me. I needed to know everything. "Peter, you need to tell me where you were. I can't go through this again."

"I can't, Lilly. Can you please just trust me on this?"

Before I could protest, Peter had his body pressed close to mine. Looking up into his green eyes, I couldn't help but see the torment inside them. I wasn't sure what his reason was for leaving town, but whatever it was, I knew it was tearing at him. Placing my hand on his cheek, I lifted to my toes and gently kissed him on the lips. The minute I felt his touch, I was no longer angry with him. All I wanted was him. There was nothing that I could do when he wrapped his arms around me and lifted my body onto the desk. Our kiss deepened as I heard the faint noise of objects falling to the floor. Peter's tongue began sweeping the inside of my mouth, massaging it with his warmth. He pulled my arms from around his neck and placed them in front of me as he lowered my body onto the desk. More items began tumbling to the floor as he made room for my body to rest.

His lips were upon mine again as he lifted my arms above my head. Lowering his mouth, he began trailing hot passionate kisses down my neck to my chest until he rested his needy mouth on my aroused nipple. Even though my breasts were covered, I could feel the hardness of my taut buds push against the material of my dress. With one hand holding my hands above my head, his other hand found the clasp of my dress behind my neck and unfastened it. My breasts sprang free with delight. The light through the window showed Peter all he needed to see. "God, you're beautiful, Lilly," he said as his sweet kisses caressed my skin.

He slowly began kissing and sucking my nipple while his free hand began caressing the other. With my hands restrained by his grip, I was unable to touch him. All I wanted was to touch him. "Peter, let me touch you," I breathed, pleading with him to let me go.

"I can't, Lilly, not yet," he said firmly.

His free hand began to wander lower down my body, lifting the material of my gown until it was bunched up around my waist. I was thankful that I decided on the black garters and stockings. I could feel his hand press against my sex as he gently began pushing his fingers inside me. "God, you feel so good," he said, pushing deeper inside me. "You are so wet, Lilly. It makes me want to fuck you right now, knowing I do this to you."

"Please, Peter, I need you inside me," I began pleading with him as my climax began to take hold.

"Not yet, baby, but soon."

I breathed out a moan of frustration. I pressed against him as he pushed another finger inside me. As his fingers pumped deeper inside me, I could feel the pressure begin to build. Just when I was about to lose it, he pulled away. He tightened the grip on my hands and pulled my body off of the desk. My heels hit the floor, and Peter placed his hands on my hips. "Turn around, baby, and lean over the desk."

I have never been one to take orders, but I was so wound up with the need to release that I could only do as he commanded. Leaning over, I pressed my body against the cold surface. Shocked by the coldness, my nipples began to harden to the point of being painful. I could feel Peter's hands on me. When he ran his hands down the curve of my ass, I heard the sound of my lacy thong being torn away. Instinct set in, and I began pushing my hips against him. I could feel the hardness of his cock through the thin fabric of his slacks. What was he waiting for? Clearly, he wanted this as much as I did.

Shifting to my elbows, I turned my head. He was just standing there gazing out the office window. "Peter, are you going to fuck me or what?" I asked with a hint of frustration.

When he finally looked at me, he said, "We better go before they find out we're missing."

Peter backed away, pulling down my gown. If I weren't so utterly confused, I would have been pissed. Taking the ends of the straps hanging below my breasts, I reached around my neck and fastened the clasp. I had finally realized what was happening. For whatever reason, Peter just blew me off. This was not going to work. "Do you mind explaining what just happened?"

Picking up my clutch from the floor, Peter graciously handed it to me, saying, "This was a mistake, Lilly. I shouldn't have brought you up here."

"Are you kidding me? You're the one who wanted us to try again, and now you're saying it was a mistake." My body was fuming. Never had any man pulled away from me right in the middle of sex.

"You're right, Lilly. I'm sorry. Maybe we need to step back," Peter said, running his hands through his hair.

"This is fucking unbelievable. I'm out of here." I was beyond pissed. How could I have been so stupid to think that this time things would be different between us?

Turning the lock on the door, I left Peter stewing in his thoughts. My head was spinning. There was no way I would wait for the elevator to arrive and chance Peter attempting to stop me. My feet kept walking as I pushed open the door to the stairwell. It didn't bother me that I was wearing five-inch heels. All I wanted to do was say my goodbyes and leave.

# CHAPTER ELEVEN
## *Lilly*

Halfway home, I was finally able to calm down. I could have kicked myself for letting a man get to me like that. I should never have agreed to take another run at our relationship. The cab I took from Tetralogy pulled up to my building forty-five minutes later. Even though Dylan was upset that I was leaving so early, the excuse I gave her about not feeling well seemed to work. I told her I would get with her tomorrow and maybe we could do lunch or something. For right now, all I wanted was to drink until I was numb and passed out.

After changing into something more comfortable, I went to find my bottle of vodka. I poured a good portion in a glass of ice and started on my journey to oblivion. I was well on my way when I heard a knock at the door. Stumbling from the couch, I opened the door without looking to see who it was. There he was, standing in front of me, looking like he had been through the wringer. His tie was undone and hanging around his neck. His tuxedo shirt was no longer crisp, but still looked good on him nonetheless. He was holding his jacket over his shoulder with his index finger. When I looked into his eyes, I could see something dark was hiding beneath them.

"What do you want, Peter? You made it perfectly clear that we were done," I said, slurring my words.

"I don't know, Lilly. All I know is that I can't stop thinking about you. No matter how dangerous it is for you to be with me, I can't stop," he said with his green eyes fixed on mine.

As I lost my balance, Peter grabbed me around the waist to steady me. "Get your hands off me, Peter. I don't need you." Even though this wasn't true, I couldn't let him know how I truly felt.

"Lilly, you're drunk. Let me help you."

"I don't need your help." I must have drunk a little more than I should have because no sooner than I said those words, I began feeling light-headed. The whole room began spinning faster and faster until I lost focus.

Peter must have taken me to my room. When I opened my eyes, I was staring at the white ceiling. I wasn't sure what time it was, but Peter was sleeping on the small chair I had in the corner of my room. He couldn't have been very comfortable considering his body was contorted in such a way that he looked like a badly-made pretzel. My stomach began to rumble, and I could feel the onset of my hangover beginning. Unable to hold the bile rising in my throat, I scrambled out of bed to my bathroom. The minute I hit the toilet, the contents of my stomach spilled into the white bowl.

I could feel my body begin to get clammy as dry heaves started to set in. Standing, I made my way to the sink and splashed some cold water on my face. Looking in the mirror, Peter was standing in the doorway with his arms crossed at his massive chest. I grabbed the washcloth hanging on the hook and wiped my face off. By the time I looked up, he was gone. I quickly brushed my teeth and headed back to bed. As I was climbing into bed, Peter reappeared with a glass of water and two pain relievers.

Handing them to me, he said, "Take these. It will make you feel better."

When I had the tablets down, along with the glass of water, I looked up to him and said, "Thank you," before I crawled back under my covers. The last thing I wanted was for Peter to see me this way. More than that, I hated the fact that I liked him taking care of me.

~****~

The morning came in with a crash. My head was pounding, and my mouth felt like a dust storm had made its way inside. Rolling over, I could see that it was 9:00 a.m. At least I hadn't slept the whole morning away. When I got out of bed and did my thing in the bathroom, it occurred to me that I could smell the aroma of coffee. I knew that I was too drunk to have remembered to set the timer on the coffee maker, so it only meant one thing, Peter was still here. Pulling up my panties, I headed to the kitchen.

Peter was behind the counter, cooking what looked to be eggs. Walking up to the counter, I asked, "Why are you still here?"

It just about knocked me over when he turned around and smiled at me. "I thought I would make you my signature hangover breakfast. It's been known to cure the worst of all hangovers."

"You don't need to do that, Peter. I'm not sure I could eat anyway. Just coffee is good enough for me," I said, pulling up a stool while I watched him flip the eggs over without a spatula. Even with a massive hangover, I was well enough to take in the view of his backside. It was a sight I would never get tired of. Turning towards me, Peter placed a cup of pure heaven in front of me, along with my favorite creamer. I didn't know what was more embarrassing, the way he was looking at me or the fact that he knew I was staring at him. Taking a sip of my coffee, I kept my head lowered. It wasn't until he started talking that my attention was drawn back to him.

"Lilly, about last night," he began. "I owe you an apology. I don't want you to think that I don't care about you. It's just that I have so much shit to deal with. It's not fair to you to wait until I do."

"What's the difference, Peter? You're still blowing me off, and I get it. I'm a big girl," I said, finishing the last of my coffee.

"Don't be like that, Lilly," he said, walking around the counter to where I was sitting.

"I need to take care of this. I'm telling you this because I care about you. If it was anyone else, it wouldn't matter," he said, cradling my cheek in his hand.

Peter was leaning towards me, and I couldn't let what was about to happen, happen. Turning my face, I said in the best voice I could muster. "Goodbye, Peter."

The way he looked at me told me that he wasn't expecting what I said. Standing, I headed back to my room, locked the door, then slid down to the floor and let the tears fall. It had to be the fact that I was still hungover and feeling like shit that made me an emotional wreck. At least that was what I was telling myself.

After wallowing in my self-pity, I pushed myself from the floor and headed to the shower. I needed to get it together. Stripping from my t-shirt and panties, I turned the nozzle to the shower just as my phone began to ring. In all my nakedness, I walked back to my bedroom to grab my phone.

"Hey, girlfriend," I answered, seeing Dylan's happy face appear on my screen.

"Hey, yourself. I was just checking to see how you were feeling today. I thought maybe you might be up for lunch," Dylan asked.

"Yeah, that would be great. Where would you like to meet?" I asked, hoping it was nowhere fancy. The way I was feeling, I was in no mood to get all dressed up.

"I thought we could grab a sandwich at that little bistro I like so much."

"Perfect. How about I meet you there at one?" I suggested.

"You gotta date."

After I hung up with Dylan, I headed back to the bathroom, where the water in the shower was still running. Climbing inside, I began feeling the warmth of the water. It's amazing what a nice hot shower can do for a woman in mourning.

~****~

Dylan was already waiting for me when I arrived at the bistro. I was surprised to see that little Isaac wasn't with her. Paying the cab driver, I stepped from the car and headed toward her. I needed to do something about my lack of transportation. I sold my car when I moved to Paris. There was really no use for it with me being gone and unable to drive it.

As we entered the small restaurant, we were greeted by a young waiter. He led us to a small table in the corner. I ordered a Reuben sandwich while Dylan ordered her favorite grilled chicken on Panini bread. I had never been here, but the atmosphere was inviting. It was no wonder this was Dylan's favorite spot. While we were eating, our conversation went back and forth between Isaac, the new gallery, Dylan's successful grand opening, and how I felt.

"So, how are things between you and Peter? You guys seemed to have disappeared at the same time last night," Dylan asked.

"Peter is Peter. And nothing is going on between us, at least not anymore," I said.

"Why? I thought things were going good between you two," Dylan questioned.

"Yeah, as I said, Peter is Peter. Too many secrets. He keeps telling me he has stuff to deal with, but he won't let me know what it is. Until he can, I can't be with someone who hides things," I said regretfully. "So how are things at The Castle? Any new sex positions or toys I needed to know about?"

"Lilly, I know you disagree with our lifestyle, but it is what makes us happy. When Rade controls me, it's like nothing I can ever explain. I trust him. He would never do anything to hurt me," Dylan confided.

"Well, I just don't understand the reason behind the whole BDSM scene."

"Lilly, you can't tell me that you haven't thought about being tied up or blindfolded during sex," Dylan whispered, leaning over towards me so no one else could hear.

"No, not really." I, of course, lied. Sometimes I did think about it, giving a man complete control over me. When I was with Peter, and he held my hands above my head, all I could think about was the way he made my body feel, knowing he was controlling my pleasure.

"Well, don't knock it until you try it, Lilly. It isn't what you think."

Leaving the restaurant, I began to think about what Dylan said about giving over control to a man in the bedroom. It was something that I only fantasized about, but never really followed through with. All I could think about was what could happen if things went wrong. I remember back when Dylan first went to The Castle. Even though Rade had nothing to do with what happened to her, I couldn't even imagine what she went through, being tied to a spanking bench and taken without the ability to fight back.

The driver pulled up to my building, distracting me from my thoughts. Paying the driver, I moaned to myself as I gave him a twenty. I really needed to buy a car.

Even though it was Sunday, I felt like I needed to get some work done. I didn't want to stay in the apartment, so I decided to go to the gallery and check how things were going with the remodel. Grabbing yet another cab, I headed out.

## CHAPTER TWELVE
*Lilly*

Arriving at the new gallery, I could see that the guys were busy working away. I requested that they work around the clock to get the gallery up and running. Unfortunately, that meant working on Sundays. I wasn't a slave driver usually, but I was so far behind on my target opening date that I had no other option but to request that they work on Sundays until the remodel was finished.

My heart sang as I looked up. Over the double glass doors, the sign 'Séduire Art Gallery' appeared in beautiful silver lettering. I hadn't expected the signage to be here so quickly, but it was now official. My dream of owning my own gallery was coming to life. As I pulled the door open, I could see men working on putting down the new flooring and adding the extra rooms that would be my office and a small conference room. If everything went as planned, I could open the new gallery in a couple of weeks. Taking a look around, I could also see that the banister leading to the second floor had been replaced with a wood and brushed silver one I had chosen. Everything was coming together. I could now see the showroom area taking shape. I was delighted with the way things were going.

When I left the gallery, I felt better. Even though I didn't like how things ended with Peter and me, I needed to push my feeling towards him away. The only way to do that was to meet someone else. I thought about the guy at the gym. I wondered if he would be around today. The only way to find out was to go. A good workout would do me good.

I arrived at the gym an hour later. Just like every other time, the place was in full swing. I decided to do some warm-up exercises, starting with a slow jog on the treadmill. While I was jogging, I looked around the gym to see if I could spot the gorgeous hunk of a man. The only thing I spotted was half-naked men showing off their chest and ab muscles. It was no surprise that the majority of the gym population was made up of horny women.

After finishing my warm-up, I decided to go to the weight room and get some reps in. Just as I was rounding the corner, I spotted him. Walking to the weight machine next to him, I acted like I didn't notice him. I knew he saw me. I could feel his eyes on me. Adjusting the weights, I looked over at him and smiled.

"Hey, Pierre, right?" I said nonchalantly, hoping he wouldn't see that I was attracted to him.

"Yeah. How are you doing, Lilly?" he asked with that beautiful smile.

"Good. Great, as a matter of fact," I said.

"Do you need help with that?" he offered.

"Yeah, that would be great," I said, watching him pull the pin from the weight stack. My eyes were glued to him. Even though he was wearing a t-shirt, it was tight enough that I could see the muscles in his arms and chest expand as he checked to make sure the weight wouldn't be too heavy for me.

"I think that should be a good weight for you," he confirmed.

I got in position on the bench. Pierre was standing behind me while I placed my hands around the bar. Even from this position, he was gorgeous. I didn't know if I would be able to concentrate on the task at hand with him standing there. Just as I was about to dislodge the weight bar from its stand, I could feel another presence. Lifting my head, I saw Peter standing in front of the bench. I released the bar and sat up.

"Is there something I can help you with, Peter?" I asked coldly.

"Can I speak with you for a moment?" he began. "In private."

Turning towards Pierre, I swung my leg around and pushed my body from the bench. "I'll be right back. This should only take a minute."

Peter grabbed my arm and escorted me out of the weight room, down the hall to an open office. Pulling me inside, he closed the door behind us. Looking down at me, he asked, "Do you mind telling me who that is?"

I could see the anger in his eyes as his grip on me began to tighten. "Not that it's any of your business, but his name is Pierre." I looked back at him in annoyance while trying to get away from him.

"Well, I don't like him, and it is my business where you are concerned. I don't want you hanging around with him," Peter spat, running his fingers through his hair.

"What is it with you? You were the one who wanted to break things off between us. Now you come in with your alpha-male bullshit and tell me who I can't hang around with. It doesn't work that way, Peter. You have no say in who I can or cannot see." I was fuming. Who the hell did he think he was?

I tried walking past Peter to escape the room, but he took hold of me once again. "What do you know about him, Lilly?"

"I was just about to find out until you so rudely interrupted me. Now let go of me," I said.

"Not until you promise me you'll steer clear of him," Peter advised.

"Whatever, Peter." I wasn't about to let him tell me what to do, but if it meant he would let me go, I would have said anything.

By the time I finished with Peter and went back to the weight room, Pierre was already gone. I tried looking for him, but he was nowhere to be found. My desire to work out left, as well. Grabbing my bag from the women's locker room, I slung it over my shoulder and left the gym. On the walk home, I thought about the altercation with Peter. I wasn't sure what his deal was, but I was tired of him running hot and cold. As much as I wanted to be with him, I couldn't wait until he got his shit together, only to find that he had moved on to some other bimbo.

~****~

Going to bed early was something I rarely did, so it was no surprise that I was wide awake at four o'clock in the morning. My body had been through the wringer yesterday, and all that it craved was a long, restful sleep. I contemplated just lying there, staring into the darkness, or getting out of bed and doing some work. With everything on track for the gallery's opening next week, there really wasn't very much left to be done. Pushing myself from the bed, I decided to go ahead and shower and grab a coffee and a bagel from the nearby Starbucks. As I was slipping on my shoes, my phone began to ring. The number came up on the screen as one I didn't recognize. If I had been smart, I would have let it go to voice mail, but being who I was, I went ahead and answered it.

It was the same as always. Silence. Just as I was ready to hang up, I heard one word spoken by the caller, "Mine."

I thought I might have misunderstood what the caller said. "Excuse me," I said as I waited for a response.

The caller hung up without saying anything else. Whoever was calling me, at least now I knew it was a man. With little battery life left, I plugged my cell into the charger and headed out of my condo in route for the coffee and bagel I could already taste.

Getting to the corner Starbucks, I entered the busy coffee shop and placed my order. Even though the place was busy, it only took a few minutes before my coffee and bagel were ready. I decide to stay and enjoy my breakfast. There was a table facing the window to the street, which I snatched and took a seat. My meal looked amazing as I began to unfold the wrapper around my bagel. I was just about to take a bite when a familiar voice said, "Mind if I join you?"

Looking up, I could see Pierre standing before me dressed in a perfectly tailored gray suit. I had to blink twice before my eyes accepted his presence. "Sure," I said, covering my full mouth with my hand. The last thing I needed was to spit food on his expensive suit.

Pierre grabbed a chair from a nearby table and pulled it next to mine. Placing his coffee and muffin on the table, he made himself comfortable.

Now that I had a clear airway, it was only right to apologize for yesterday. "I'm sorry about yesterday. Sometimes Peter can be a little rude."

"It's okay. So, is this Peter guy, your boyfriend?" Pierre asked casually.

With a chuckle, I said, "I'm not sure what he is, but my boyfriend isn't one of them."

"Well, then maybe it won't be too forward of me to ask you to dinner," Pierre asked with a smile.

"I'd like that," I replied.

Pierre walked me out of the coffee shop and down the sidewalk towards my condo. We stopped just outside my building. Pierre took hold of my hand and squeezed it lightly. I cast my attention to him, only to see him lowering his head to mine. Just when I thought he would kiss me on the lips, he gently kissed my forehead. "I'll see you tomorrow night, Lilly," he said before turning and walking away.

He left my body quivering as I watched Pierre leave. There was definitely something mysterious about him that I wouldn't mind getting to know. Turning, I headed back up to my condo. When I got to my floor, Cop was knocking on my door. I wasn't sure why he would be knocking on my door. I really didn't have anything to say to him. I knew that Peter still had his men watching me. Even though I couldn't see them, I could feel them around.

Stepping up to him with my keys in my hand, I asked, "Is there something you needed?"

"Good morning, Lilly. Peter sent me over to check on you. When you didn't answer your phone, he got worried," Cop explained, moving aside so I could unlock my door.

"Well, you can tell Peter that I'm alive and well," I said sarcastically.

"Do you mind if I check out your condo?" he asked.

"Yes, I mind. You need to tell Peter he needs to back off."

"I'm not to leave until I've checked to make sure it's safe," he demanded.

"What is it with you, guys?" I complained as I waved my hand up and down.

With no other choice, I let Cop enter my home so he could look around. In the meantime, I removed my phone from the charger and called Peter. "What the hell is your problem?"

"Maybe you should answer your phone when I call you," he said.

"Maybe you should stop being so paranoid and let me be."

"I can't do that, Lilly. Until I can figure out what the calls are about, I'm going to keep you safe," Peter stated.

"You are so frustrating," I said, before I hung up on him.

Cop finished his inspection of my condo, leaving me agitated by Peter's insistence on having him look around. The more I thought about it, the angrier I got. I needed to stop letting this man get to me and focus on something else. I decided to do an Internet search to see if I could locate any good deals on a car. My parents purchased my last car, so I wasn't even sure how much a new car would cost. Even though I didn't budget for a car, it was something that I desperately needed. I wasn't one to take the subway, and taking a taxi was beginning to put a hole in my wallet.

After spending most of my time looking for a new car and not really knowing what to look for, I called my dad to see if he could offer any advice. I was pleasantly surprised to find that he offered to take care of it. He basically knew what

I wanted, so it wasn't a problem for him to find a good dealer.

Besides finding transportation, the only thing I had planned today was going to the gallery and checking on things. Even though I had just gone yesterday, I was beginning to get anxious. I wanted to have it completed so I could start doing my thing.

~****~

When I arrived at the gallery, the men were busy working away. I found the foreman for the construction crew and stepped up to him. I needed to find out when he expected everything to be completed so that I could have my opening. He assured me that everything would be ready by the end of the week. This was perfect; it would give me enough time to get the announcements out and get everything ready. My office was pretty much, already finished. All I needed to do was to purchase some furniture and a new computer.

Since everything seemed to be under control, I decided to head over to the IKEA store to see what I could find to furnish my new office. The forty-five-minute ride was well worth it. I found everything I needed and set up a delivery time for Friday. While I waited for the store associate to complete my order, I looked on-line for computer equipment. Within minutes I found what I needed and ordered it with a rush delivery to the gallery. Thinking about the technical stuff, it wouldn't hurt to find an IT person to take care of hooking up my computers and whatever he or she thought would be necessary for the business. It was getting late, so this task would need to wait until tomorrow.

By the time I got home, my feet ached, and I was ready to just veg out on my couch and watch a good movie. I didn't feel much like cooking either, so I called for Chinese food from one of my favorite places. I kept thinking about how much I hated spending time alone. It seemed as if I was doing that a lot lately. It was then that I decided to see if Brie was home. Since we couldn't meet up a few days ago, maybe she wanted to do a movie and Chinese food with me. I didn't have her number, so I decided to walk across the hall to see if she was home.

After knocking on her door several times, I finally gave up and headed back to my condo. I left her a note letting her know to come over when she got home if it wasn't too late. I wasn't sure what her schedule was at the coffee shop, but I would assume she wouldn't be working too much later since it was already approaching eight o'clock. I didn't think people would be drinking coffee at this hour.

I must have been a lot more tired than I thought because when I woke up, there was another movie on, and my food, which I barely touched, was cold. Stumbling off the couch, I decided that my bed would be a lot more comfortable than the couch. Fifteen minutes later, I was snuggled beneath my covers, ready for sleep to take over. It wasn't long after my head hit the pillow that I was out.

# CHAPTER THIRTEEN
## *Lilly*

The sun was shining brightly through my bedroom blinds, letting me know that morning had hit. I had a lot of things that I needed to take care of today. In a couple of days, the furniture would be delivered to the gallery, and I didn't have much time left to get things ready for the opening. The contractor assured me that everything would be ready by the end of the week, giving me only a couple of days to get the word out. More than anything, I wanted everything ready by Saturday.

My morning was spent at the gallery working with the IT guy from Tetralogy that Dylan offered to assist me. After he set everything up, I was finally up and running. Brie was supposed to stop by after her shift so I could show her how to work the system and get her up to speed on what I wanted her to do.

I had been so busy with Brie that I lost track of time. Pierre was going to meet me at 7:00 p.m. for our dinner date, and I wasn't even close to being finished at the gallery. I didn't have a way to get in touch with him, seeing how I neglected to get his number. There was no way I could tell him that I would need to cancel. The only thing I could do was head to my condo and hope that I would have enough time to shower and be ready for him by seven o'clock.

By the time I got to my condo, it was 6:30 p.m. I only had thirty minutes to shower and dress before he showed up. Striping my clothes off one piece at a time, I headed to the bathroom. I thought this was the best way to save time. Even though there was now a trail of clothing lining the floor leading to the bathroom, I was fully naked and ready for a quick shower.

~****~

Right on time, Pierre was waiting for me as I exited the elevator. He looked very casual in a black pair of jeans, a gray t-shirt, and a black jacket. His hair was a little bit tossed, like he may have just stepped out of the shower himself. It was still a really good look on him. Better than good. As I walked up to him, I could feel his eyes burning into me. I wasn't sure if he was looking at me because I may have been a little overdressed or because he was just as attracted to me as I was to him.

Lifting to my tiptoes, I placed my hands on his shoulders and placed a warm kiss on his cheek. "Hey," I said, lowering my heels to the ground.

"You look great," he complimented, taking my hands in his. "Are you ready?"

Nodding, I said, "Yes."

When we stepped outside, a silver Tesla was parked at the curb. When he opened the passenger side for me, I knew it was his. I wasn't sure what he did for a living, but he must have had a pretty good job to afford such an expensive car. Buckling in, I looked his way and asked, "So where are we going for dinner?"

"I thought we would go to the NoMad Hotel. They have one of the best restaurants in the city if that's okay with you," he said.

"That would be wonderful," I replied, moving my focus to the street as he pulled from the curb.

A short time later, we were in front of the hotel. A valet was waiting to park the car as we stopped. I had never been to this hotel, but I heard some very good things about it. Pierre rounded the car as the valet assisted me out. Once outside the vehicle, Pierre took my hand and guided me inside. Even though it was built in the early 1900s, the English-style decor was very attractive.

As we reached the hotel's restaurant, an attractive hostess was waiting to seat us. As we followed her, I could feel the eyes of the other patrons upon us. Mostly the women were staring at us. It made me wonder if it was because of envy or jealousy. Pierre being a very handsome man, my guess was jealousy. The hostess stopped in front of a table for two in the back. Even though it was still a part of the restaurant, it was hidden away from the rest of the tables, making it very private and cozy. I wondered if Pierre had to pay extra to get this table.

Looking at the menu, it didn't surprise me that it was one of the top-rated restaurants in New York. Everything on the menu sounded delicious. Pierre must have seen my indecisiveness because he gently took hold of my hand and squeezed it gently, saying, "How about I order for you?"

"That would be great. I'm not sure what to order," I replied.

The waiter came and took our orders. I knew no matter what Pierre ordered for me, it would be amazing. Taking a sip of my wine, he asked, "So what brought you to New York?"

Placing my glass on the linen-covered table, I responded with a smile, "I actually just got back from Paris. I'm opening a new art gallery."

"An art gallery, how wonderful. Maybe I could stop by and see it," he said.

"That would be great. I'm hoping to have an opening next Saturday. I would love for you to come."

As the night went on, I found out some amazing things about him. I learned that we had more in common than I initially thought. I discovered that he was originally from Paris, and he was interested in opening a design company in

New York. By the time we finished dinner, I knew more about him than I knew about Peter. There was something about him that seemed too good to be true. No one could be that perfect and have the same interests as me.

It was getting late, and I needed to get home. I had a full day tomorrow dealing with the contractors and the delivery of the new furniture. I also still had a few things to iron out with the computer system. When we pulled up to my building, I was ready to say goodbye, but Pierre insisted on walking me to my door. Standing in front of him, the awkwardness began to filter in.

"Thank you for a wonderful dinner. I really enjoyed myself." Before I could finish thanking him, his lips were on mine. His tender touch had my body tingling all the way to my core. My lips parted, allowing him access to my warmth. As our tongues danced together, I could feel the hardness of his erection push against me as he pulled me closer to him. "*Mon chéri, qu'est-ce que tu fais pour moo?*"

"*Idem,*" I said. I wasn't sure what he was doing to me either, but I wanted more.

Breaking the kiss, he looked down on me. When I finally opened my eyes, I could see his brilliant smile as he brushed his thumb across my lips. "I better go before I can't stop. When can I see you again?"

Pulling a pen from my small purse, I took hold of his hand, flipped it over so that his palm was face up, and wrote my number down. Without another word, I turned and unlocked my door, and went inside. Leaning against it, I placed my finger on my lips and smiled to myself.

## CHAPTER FOURTEEN
### *Lilly*

Two more days and the opening of Séduire Art Gallery would happen. I had worked my ass off, trying to get everything ready. The furniture arrived, and it looked perfect in the gallery. There were a couple of problems with the lighting, but thankfully, the contractor could fix it in no time. All the caterers had been called, and they would be here in time to set up for the opening taking place at 5:00 p.m. Now the only thing to worry about was how many people would be actually showing up.

Sitting in my office, I heard the ringing of the door chime. Pushing my chair from my desk, I went to see who had entered. Standing just outside my door, my stomach began to twist as Peter's gorgeous body appeared. I took in a deep breath. I didn't know what he was doing here. I hadn't seen him in a week. I thought for sure he was away taking care of whatever shit he needed to. Brushing my hands down my skirt to straighten out the wrinkles, I headed to the gallery's showroom area. Peter was standing in front of one of my favorite black and white pictures taken by a well-known photographer. Even though I typically didn't like this form of art, he was an exception to the rule. I thought it would be nice to dedicate one section of the gallery to his photos.

Walking up behind Peter, I said softly, "Amazing, isn't it?"

Turning towards me, Peter placed his hand on my cheek and said, "It certainly is."

"What are you doing here, Peter?" I asked, stepping back a couple of feet.

"I needed to talk to you," he stated with a serious look on his face.

"Okay. So talk."

"Is there somewhere we can go?" he asked.

"There's no one else here, Peter. Just say what you have to say," I said, looking around the room.

"There's something you need to know about that guy from the gym. He isn't who you think he is, Lilly."

"If you are talking about Pierre, I know everything I need to know about him, which is more than I can say about you." Even though it was the truth, I regretted saying the words when there was a change of expression on Peter's face.

"Well, that may be, but at least I don't have a criminal record, Lilly. Did you know he has a record for raping a girl?" Peter began moving closer, with a sudden change in his demeanor.

"What are you talking about, Peter, and why are you looking into Pierre, anyway?"

"There was something about him that didn't sit well with me, so I checked into him," he admitted. "He's dangerous, Lilly."

"I can't listen to this anymore." I didn't know what to think. I wasn't even sure if I could believe what he was saying. For all I knew, he didn't want any man near me as long as there was a chance for us to be together. Backing away from him, I turned to head back to my office. My progress was abruptly stopped when his hand took hold of my arm. Stopped in my tracks, I turned to face him. "We're done talking, Peter."

"Lilly, no matter what you think, I will always care about you. I'm asking that you please listen to me, no matter how you feel about me." Peter's eyes showed his sincere concern.

It didn't matter what I felt for Peter; it was written all over my face the minute he looked at me with those eyes. When his grip on my arm softened, and he took me into his arms, nothing could change the way I felt about him. It didn't matter that his need to protect me was over the top or that he had secrets he was keeping from me. All that mattered was the way he made me feel at that very moment. Studying him closely, his head lowered to mine, and his lips were suddenly on mine. The tingle began the minute he parted my lips and began twisting his tongue with mine. I was so absorbed in the here and now that I had no control over myself. My hands wrapped around his neck as I pulled him even closer yet. My body floated upward, feeling his hands lower and swoop me into his arms. He must have known where to take me because before I knew it, I was on the leather couch in my office with Peter hovering over me.

All I could think about was having him. Taking the hem of his t-shirt, I lifted the soft material up over his head, exposing his masculine chest. Every line of his hard body was on display. Kissing my way down his perfection, I undid the buckle on his belt and ripped it from his jeans. Peter grabbed his belt from me and coiled it around my wrists. Just as I was about to protest, he whispered. "I would never hurt you, Lilly."

Letting him continue, I was suddenly bound to the chrome armrest on the leather couch. Having left me unable to move my hands, Peter began slowly unbuttoning my silk blouse while kissing his way down my sensitized body. Only his touch could make me feel this way. "Peter," I moaned, feeling he knew exactly what I wanted.

"Just feel, baby," he whispered.

My breasts were completely exposed to him as he unfastened the clasp of my bra. In a nanosecond, his mouth was on my nipple, kissing and sucking it into a hard peak. He knew exactly what drove me crazy with desire for him.

Reaching under my skirt, his hand began moving to my core. I could feel the wetness building as his hands skimmed closer and closer to my slick folds. As he inserted one and then another finger, I was lost. The rush of pleasure hit at once. My body was no longer my own. It was his.

Pulling his jeans down the rest of the way, Peter took special care as he entered my tight channel. As he pumped his cock in and out of me, I could feel the onset of another orgasm when he changed his position so that he was now hitting my g-spot. He thrust further inside me, and my heart began to beat faster while my breathing became more erratic. I no longer had the strength to hold back. Electricity filled my body as my need to release finally won. It wasn't until I was coming down from the explosion that I felt the spasm of Peter inside me. He, too, had met his delivery.

"Peter, we have to stop doing this," I panted, not knowing why I would want to stop something that felt so good.

"I can't, Lilly. I have to be with you," he said.

"Then tell me what is going on with you." If he would just tell me the truth, we could be together. If he would just open up to me, then we could deal with it and move forward.

"I can't. Not yet." Peter said, pulling his semi-hard cock from inside me.

The minute he pulled away, I knew whatever he was keeping from me was tearing him apart. I lifted my body from the couch and began straightening out my rumpled clothing. Looking up at the door, Peter was standing outside facing me. Tucking my blouse in my skirt, I asked, "Where are you going?"

"There's something I need to do. Cop is parked out front, and Josh is out back. I'll be back in a few hours to take you home."

~****~

I wasn't sure what was going on with Peter. The last couple of days had been weird, to say the least. The last time I saw him was when he drove me home two days ago. His only communication with me was by cell and text. I kept thinking about what he said about Pierre. If it was true and

Pierre did rape a girl, why hadn't he made a move towards me? The only contact we had was kissing. It just didn't make sense.

Tonight at the opening, somehow I needed to find out if what Peter said was true. I needed to confront Pierre about it, but I needed to be careful about how I asked him. The last thing I wanted was to upset him.

Focusing on something else, I walked to the kitchen and poured myself a cup of coffee. Taking my coffee with me, I placed it on the bathroom counter as I filled the tub full of water. I needed to get a move on if I wanted to get to the gallery to finalize the opening's remaining details.

Brie had already sorted out the details with the caterers. We both had worked hard to get all of the displays ready for the opening. My only hope was that the opening would bring some avid collectors, and some of the pieces could be sold.

It was approaching late morning, and I needed to head out to the gallery. To save time, I thought it would be easier to get ready at the gallery instead of at the condo. Placing my dress in a garment bag, I grabbed it along with my needed essentials and headed to the parking garage. Just like my father promised, a shiny new Lexus was delivered yesterday. He assured me he got a good deal on it. When I offered to pay him for the car, he insisted that what I did for him in Paris with that gallery was payment enough.

Tossing my things in the back seat, I pulled out onto 5th Avenue and headed to the gallery. It was so nice being able to come and go as I pleased without having to hail a cab. Looking out my rearview mirror, I could see that Peter was following me in his Camaro. The calls I was getting had stopped; at least, I hadn't received any since my dinner with Pierre.

I drove around the back of the gallery and parked the Lexus in the parking spot closest to the back door. Gathering my things, I looked around, hoping to see Peter, but he was nowhere around. I could only assume that he must be staked out in front. Walking through the back entrance, I could hear the subtle sound of violin music playing, letting me know the musicians had arrived and were warming up. The music they played was very soothing, and something the guests would enjoy while looking at the art. I had to hand it to Brie, for someone who didn't know that much about art, she was beginning to fit right in. It was like she had a gift for putting things together and making them perfect.

Before I headed to my office, I wanted to take one more look around. I placed my things on the reception counter and headed up the stairs. Brie made last minute adjustments to the lighting, making sure every angle of the paintings was captured perfectly.

"Hey," I said, watching her step off the step ladder.

"Oh, hey, Lilly. So, what do you think?" Brie asked, pointing to the lights above.

"I think they are set perfectly. I'm glad we went with the softer bulbs. They really bring out the colors," I replied, scanning the rest of the area. "So, it looks like everything is set. I like the music you have chosen for tonight. Now we can only pray we will have a good turnout and sell some paintings."

As the evening wore on, more and more people arrived. As I was visiting with Dylan, I felt a soft tap on my shoulder. Turning, Pierre was standing before me. God, he was gorgeous. He was dressed in a dark suit and a crisp white shirt. I don't know if it was the gallery's lighting, but his eyes were dark and mesmerizing. Dylan must have noticed my fixation on him because she bumped my shoulder with hers.

"Sorry. Dylan Matheson, this Pierre... umm," I couldn't believe that I didn't even know his last name.

"Marchand, Pierre Marchand. It's nice to meet you, Ms. Matheson," he said, taking her hand and placing a soft kiss on the back.

"Please, call me Dylan," she smiled, looking at him with the same fixation.

"So, it seems your opening is a big hit," Pierre said.

"It is. Thank you so much for coming," I returned.

"It was my pleasure. Do you mind if I steal Lilly away?" he asked, looking at Dylan.

"Not at all. Enjoy."

Pierre took hold of my hand, and we walked up the steps. I thought it would be the best place to start the tour. As we were enjoying ourselves, one waiter came along with a tray of appetizers and another with a tray of champagne. I was filled with so much excitement that I couldn't eat a bite, but the champagne offered something I needed to settle my nerves. By the time we finished our tour, Pierre had purchased several pieces of art. He knew a gentleman who would appreciate the details in the collection.

We were standing in front of a display of abstract art when Pierre softly whispered in my ear, "Is there somewhere where we can be alone?"

Taking him by the hand, I led him in the direction of my office. Once we were inside, I closed the door. "Can I get you something to drink?" I asked, walking to the credenza behind my desk.

"Whatever you're having will be fine," he said.

Pouring two tumblers with vodka, I rounded my desk and handed him one. Taking a sip, I kept my eyes on him. "Let's sit," I said, taking him by the hand and leading him to the couch. Somehow I needed to find out what happened between him and the girl he was accused of raping. Placing my glass on the glass table, I faced him. "So tell me more about yourself?"

"What's there to tell? You already know so much about me," he said.

"Well, I don't know if you have any girlfriends, I don't know if you have ever been in love," I began. "What was growing up like?"

"I had a good childhood. My parents were very loving. They gave me everything that I wanted. They insisted I have the very best. I was an only child, so you could say that they spoiled me. When I went off to college, they made sure I went to the very best. That was where I fell in love for the first time. She was American. Her parents worked for the government. We were so in love until..."

"Until what, Pierre?" I asked.

"Until her parents found out. She was two years younger than me and, by all accounts, a minor. Even though we loved each other, it didn't matter to them. They accused me of raping her. My parents did everything they could to have the charges dropped, but because her parents worked for the government, they had a lot more pull," he explained.

"So, what happened?" I asked, placing my hand on his.

"My parents ended up making a deal with them. If I agreed never to see her again, the charges would be reduced, my record sealed, and I would get no more than a slap on the hand." Pierre placed his hand over mine and tapped it lightly. "Needless to say, I transferred to a different college and never saw her again."

"That must have been horrible for you. To know that you could never be with the one you loved," I said, sympathetically.

"It was a long time ago, in the past." Pierre looked at me, taking hold of my hand and bringing it to his lips. "You remind me of her in a way."

I knew there was something mysterious about him. Now I knew what it was. Peter was wrong about what he found. It was no more than an innocent love that her parents saw as something dirty and vile. I couldn't understand if the record was sealed, how was Peter able to get the information? While I was pondering the answer, Pierre lowered his lips to mine. His kiss was soft and tender, just like the one before. I placed my hand on his shoulder and pulled him closer to me. The kiss deepened as he began twisting his tongue with mine. It was no surprise that the French really knew how to kiss. I was like putty in his arms. Before we could take our connection any further, there was a knock on my door.

Standing, I straightened my dress and walked to the door. Brie was on the other side, holding her jacket over her arm while holding a stack of invoices in the other hand. "I'm going to take off. Here are the invoices for the sales we made this evening. I can go through them on Monday if you'd like. It was a perfect night," she said, handing the stack of papers to me.

"Thank you so much for your help. I couldn't have done it without you," I admitted, taking the stack of invoices from her.

Placing the invoice on my desk, I turned toward Pierre. As much as I wanted this evening to continue, I was beat. All I wanted was my nice warm bed. Pierre must have read my mind. He stood from the couch, drinking the last of his vodka and placing the glass on the table. "It's time that I left. Can I give you a ride home?"

"Thank you, but no. I have my car here. I'll walk you out," I offered.

While I unlocked the front door, Pierre gave me a light peck on the cheek. I watched as he headed to his car. Closing the door, I turned and leaned up against it and surveyed the gallery. Only then did I realize what was happening to me. How could I have feelings for two very different men? On the one hand, Peter was strong and controlling, with secrets, while Pierre was romantic and willing to share his. How long could I continue seeing both of them before one of them got hurt?

# CHAPTER FIFTEEN
## *Lilly*

I could feel the sun shining through the blinds in my bedroom, signaling that morning was already here. After Pierre left the gallery, I finished cleaning up the remnants of the opening. Even though it ended up being a good turnout, I was glad that it was over. Jumping from my bed, I took a quick shower and pulled on a pair of workout shorts, a sports bra, and a light tank. I felt like, for once, everything was going my way. Locking the door, I headed out to Maximum Capacity to see if I could get in a quick workout before heading to the gallery. I knew I had a lot of work ahead of me going over the sales invoices. I couldn't let Brie struggle through them, knowing she had done so much for me in such a short amount of time. I thought it would be nice to give her Monday off, especially after all the hard work she did.

The air in the gym was a little lighter than usual. It didn't seem quite as crowded as it usually was for a Sunday morning. Heading to my favorite treadmill, I decided to do a quick warm-up before I tackled the weights. It would have been nice to see Pierre so I could work out with him, but he wasn't here.

Listening to my iPod, I got distracted when the treadmill suddenly slowed, and the display monitor went black. Pulling my earbuds from my ears, I turned around and saw Peter standing at the end of the treadmill holding the electrical cord in his hand. His smile was bright, and he once again looked like a Greek God.

Placing my hands on my hips, I looked over to him, annoyed. "That wasn't funny, Peter," I said.

"I needed to get your attention," he confessed, plugging the cord back into the wall.

"Okay, you got it, so what is this about?" I asked, stepping off the treadmill.

"I thought we could work out together. I could spot you," he said with a grin.

"Sure," I agreed.

We headed to the weight room; I could feel Peter watching me from behind. Taking a look to my right, I saw his face in the mirrored wall. Knowing that look, I added a little extra to my step and watched as his face lit up. I knew that it wasn't fair to lead him on in this way, but I had to admit, it was fun watching him drool.

When we finished our workout, Peter offered to buy me breakfast. I agreed since I skipped breakfast and my morning java. I suggested we go to the corner café, which was a couple of blocks from the gym. There was something that caught my attention. Looking behind me, I could have sworn I saw Pierre's car stopped at the light. I must have been seeing things because it was no longer there.

Peter must have noticed me turn. "What are you looking at?"

"It's nothing. I thought I recognized Pierre's car," I said, hesitantly.

Peter turned around right away and began to scan the area as he walked backward. He must have been satisfied. There was nothing to see because he turned again and stepped forward. "So I take it you aren't taking my advice to stay away from him."

"You were wrong about what you said about him. The rape charges were reduced. He fell in love with a girl whose parents slapped a rape charge on him only because she was a minor and he wasn't," I said defensively. "How were you able to get that information anyway? His records were sealed as long as he stayed away from her."

"I have my ways, Lilly, especially when it comes to your safety," Peter responded.

The coffee shop wasn't very busy. We took a seat at one of the booths next to the window. Our waitress took our order and brought us our coffee. I just stared at Peter as he put four packets of sugar in his cup. Stirring his coffee, he looked over to me with a smile. "I like my coffee extra sweet," he said as he took a sip.

Rolling my eyes, I replied, "I bet your dentist loves you."

"As a matter of fact, she does, especially when I bring her cream-filled donuts," he said.

I wasn't sure if he was trying to be funny, so I just ignored his comment. The waitress brought us our meal. Peter's consisted of three eggs over-easy, four strips of bacon, three dollar-sized pancakes, and a heaping mound of hash browns. Compared to my strawberry pancake with a side of cream, his meal could feed three people. I guess a man his size could put away a lot more food.

After finishing our meal, Peter insisted on walking with me back to my condo. I knew that no matter how much I protested, he wouldn't give up. When we got to the condo, my door was cracked open. I must have been losing it because I could have sworn I locked the door. As a matter of fact, I knew I had locked it.

Peter pushed me behind him and said, "Wait here, Lilly."

I nodded as I watched him slowly pushed the door further open. I stayed in the hall, wondering what was taking him so long. Unable to wait any longer, I quietly moved toward the door and entered. I didn't see Peter, so I softly whispered, "Peter, where are you?"

It was at that moment that I remembered the call I got a few days ago. I started to have second thoughts about everything. Maybe I was being stalked. Looking around, I couldn't see anything out of place. Peter appeared from the hallway. "Whoever was here, they're gone. It doesn't look like anything has been disturbed," Peter said.

"Peter, I know I locked my door. Just like the last time," I said, adamantly

"I think it would be wise to have the locks on your door changed," he said, pulling his phone from his pocket.

I knew by the tone in his voice that he was talking to one of his men. I couldn't hear the full conversation, but I got the gist of it. He was arranging for someone to come over and change the locks on my door. While Peter was finishing up with the arrangements, I walked to my room to take a much-needed shower. Stripping off my clothing, I went to my dresser to pull out a bra and underwear set. I noticed that the drawer containing my bras and panties was opened. I couldn't understand why it would be pulled out. Scanning the contents, I noticed that some items were missing. Thinking that I may have forgotten to wash them, I began going through my laundry basket. The lacy pink and black matching bra and panties weren't there.

I needed to get in the shower, so I decided on a different matching set and postponed looking for the missing items until later. Rinsing the conditioner from my hair, I heard a soft knock on the bathroom door. Turning off the faucet, I grabbed a towel and wrapped it around my body. Leaning against the door, I said, "I'll be out in a minute."

I hurried and put on my bra and panties, wrapped a towel around my wet hair, and grabbed my robe from the back of the door. I could feel that there was something in the pocket. Reaching inside, I pulled out a handful of pink rose petals. Opening the door, I held out my hand and revealed them to Peter. "Did you put these in the pocket of my robe?"

Peter looked at me, confused. "Why would I do that, Lilly?"

"Just like, why would you take my favorite bra and underwear set?" I said, agitated by his denial.

"What are you talking about, Lilly?"

Pushing past him, I dumped the rose petals in the trash and proceeded to finish getting dressed. I could feel Peter's eyes on me, waiting for an answer. Turning towards him, I began pulling on my jeans and said, "Who else could have taken them, Peter? You are the only person who has been in my bedroom."

"I didn't take your underwear, and I certainly didn't put rose pedals in your pocket," he said defensively.

Looking up at him, I could see that he was telling me the truth. The more I thought about it, there was no reason for him to take anything. "Maybe I misplaced them, but it still doesn't explain the petals."

"I'm placing someone outside your door, Lilly, 24/7. Someone is stalking you," Peter stated.

Rising from the bed, Peter walked over to where I was standing. Taking me into his arms, he began holding me tight. "I'm not going to let anything happen to you, Lilly. I'll find out who it is."

Looking up at him, our eyes met. Peter lowered his lips to mine and softly kissed me. My arms automatically wrapped around his shoulders as he lifted my body from the floor. The feel of his body so close to mine had me wanting more of him. He gently laid me on the bed and began trailing kisses down my neck and across my collarbone. Lowering the cup of my bra, his mouth consumed my breasts as his tongue flicked back and forth against my nipple. My back began to arch, needing more of what he was giving me. Trailing my hands down his broad shoulders to his muscular back, I grabbed the hem of his t-shirt and pulled it over his head. My head was filled with the scent of musk and something masculine.

I wrapped my legs around his waist as his body began to grind against mine. The feel of his erection through his shorts had me undone. Lowering my hands down his body, I pushed my fingers under his waistband and began slipping his shorts over his tight ass and down his muscular legs. Peter went to his knees and pulled my body close to his. He began working on the zipper of my jeans while I undid the clasp of my bra and tossed it to the floor. Lifting my hips, Peter pulled the fabric of my jeans down my legs and off my body.

Looking down at me, I saw his smiling face as he said, "Nice."

His hands went under my ass, tugging my lacy thong off. With my body completely naked, Peter resumed his position, placing my legs over his shoulders. His mouth began trailing wet kisses along my inner thigh, stopping just at the juncture of my sex. Pushing upward, I moved my hips so that I could feel his warm mouth on my slick folds. Peter tightened his grip on my hips, allowing him to take control of my movements. "You need to hold still, Lilly, or I'll stop," he ordered.

Not wanting him to stop, I ceased my movements and waited for him to continue his play. I would never be able to get enough of his touch. I knew the only way to get what I needed was to obey his command. Just like an obedient child, he gave me my reward. His fingers penetrated me while his mouth began circling my clit. As he lapped and sucked the hard nub, I could feel the beginning of my orgasm take control. I tried to stay still, but I needed more. My hips begin moving once again. It was only after I felt a slight sting on my ass cheek that I stopped.

"I told you not to move, Lilly. The next one won't be as gentle," he commanded.

I've never been spanked before, but there was something about his words and the feel of the sting against my cheek that made me want him to do it again. Pushing my luck, I moved my hips even more. In one swift move, I was on my stomach. Peter was holding on to my hips, pulling them up towards him. With my hips in the air, I felt the sting of his hand come down on my cheeks, first on the right, then on the left. "I think you like being punished for your misbehavior," Peter whispered.

When another slap came down on my tingling cheek, it was over. My gates opened, and I could no longer hold back my release. It was the most intense orgasm I had ever experienced. The minute my scream of pleasure rang, Peter was inside me, thrusting and driving inside with no mercy. I could feel my body climax again the deeper Peter drove into me. When my name rolled off his lips, I knew he met his pleasure as well.

We laid there motionless as our bodies began to come down. Peter was on top of me with his chest to my back—his cock still wedged inside me. As my breathing began to even out, the tears began to fall. I wasn't sure what was happening to me. Peter must have sensed something was wrong because no sooner than the tears came, his body was off of mine, and I was wrapped in his arms.

"Lilly, what is it? Did I hurt you?" he asked compassionately.

"No. That was amazing, Peter. I liked what you did to me," I said, propping up on my elbows.

Peter kissed the top of my head and pushed himself from the bed. I wasn't sure what was going on with him, but his change in mood was evident. "Where are you going?" I asked, confused.

"I need to get to the hardware store so we can change your locks," he claimed, pulling his jeans on.

"Right now? You have to do it now?" I asked.

"No better time than the present."

Before I could get off the bed, he was already out the door. I wasn't sure what just happened. All I knew was it had to stop.

## CHAPTER SIXTEEN
### *Lilly*

Peter never came back to my condo after leaving so quickly. Just like before, I hadn't seen him for a couple of days. I tried calling him several times, but my calls always went to voice mail. Even my conversation with Cop led nowhere. At least I knew he was alive. The locks on my door were changed, and an extra deadbolt was placed on the door, all evident by the new set of keys lying on my kitchen counter next to a note saying,

*"Here are your new keys. Please make sure all three locks are secure when you leave. PH."*

I spent the whole day at the gallery thinking about Peter and needing to speak with him. I knew there would be a good chance that he would be at the gym. Gathering my bag and making sure all the doors were locked, I walked to my car. Just as I opened the door, I heard Pierre's voice behind me.

"Lilly, wait," he yelled from the alley.

Stopping, I turned and waited for him to reach me. When he got close enough, I said, "Hi, Pierre, I'm kind of in a hurry."

"I thought we could grab a bite to eat," he offered.

"It will need to be some other time. I really need to go." As much as I wanted to go with him, it was really a bad time. This thing with Peter was something that I really needed to take care of.

"Wait," he began, "Where are you going? Maybe we could meet after you take care of what you need to."

"I'm going to the gym. I really need to speak to Peter." I'm not sure why I told him of my plans, but I felt that he should know.

"Are you back together with him?" Pierre questioned, with what looked like an angry look in his eyes. "Is that why you were with him, having breakfast?"

"How did you know about that?" I asked.

"I saw you with him the other day. I saw you walk into that café with him," Pierre admitted.

"So, I did see you the other day, in your car? Were you following me?"

"Of course not," Pierre declared, becoming even more angry.

"Pierre, I really need to go. Can I get a rain check?" I asked.

"Of course. I'll call you later," he said.

Looking back at him in my rearview mirror, I could see his demeanor had changed. His hands were balled into fists like he was ready to hit something or someone. Maybe I didn't know him as well as I thought.

When I got to the gym, it didn't surprise me that the place was packed. Since I was in a hurry to get there, I didn't change into my workout clothes. Heading to the woman's locker room, I scanned the area to see if I could see Peter. I knew that if he were here, he would be working in the weight room, which was on the other side of the gym. I decided to change first and then head there.

Even though the weight room was packed with hard bodies, not one of them belonged to Peter. As much as I was disappointed not to find him here, I decided to work out my frustrations on the indoor running track. After a couple of times around the track, I learned that even running in circles couldn't pacify my frustration. Calling it quits, I headed back to the locker room to take a quick shower and head home.

Cop was still standing in front of my door when I got to the condo. He must be really dedicated to his job, I thought to myself. Why else would anyone stand in front of a door for hours on end? Moving past him without a word, I took the keys from my bag and began unlocking the locks. I swung the door open and stepped inside. Before I closed it, I saw Pierre walking towards me with a beautiful bouquet of flowers. I opened the door wider, so he could see me.

"Lilly," he began. "I came to apologize for my behavior earlier," he said, giving Cop an evil look.

I stepped aside so he could enter. Facing him, I said, "You didn't need to come all the way here just to apologize."

"I felt it was necessary to do it face to face," Pierre said, leaning towards me and placing a soft kiss on my cheek. "These are for you."

Taking the flowers from him, I walked to the kitchen to locate a vase. Finally finding one, I filled it full of water and placed the bouquet of pink roses in the vase. Looking over to where he was standing, I asked, "Would you like a glass of wine?"

He turned to face me. "I would love one. Who's the guy?" he asked.

"Nobody," I said, not wanting to go into detail as to why Cop was standing in front of my door.

Grabbing two glasses from the cupboard, I filled them half-full with wine. I walked over to where he was standing by the window and handed him his wine. "Let's sit," I said, taking him by the hand.

"So, how about that rain check?" Pierre asked.

"I don't feel much like going out," I admitted.

"Well, how about we order in?" Pierre suggested.

"Okay, I think I have some menus for takeout in the kitchen. Is there anything you prefer?" I ask, pushing myself to my feet.

"Whatever you like is fine," he said.

Grabbing my phone from my bag, I called the Italian place we decided on. As I looked at my phone, I could see that I had missed a call from Peter. I was just about ready to return his call when I decided it was better if I let him stew. After all, I had been calling him for two days with no answer. Placing our order, I grabbed the wine bottle and sat next to Pierre. Filling our glasses, I tipped the glass to my lips and drank half of its contents. Looking over to Pierre, I said, "I think we are going to need another bottle."

I had no care in the world by the time our delivery order showed up. Pierre handed the delivery guy a hundred dollar bill and told him to keep the change. The meal went by in a complete blur. I knew I drank quite a bit of wine, but my head wasn't normally this foggy. Standing up to take our empty plates to the kitchen, I stumbled backward. Pierre's hands wrapped around my body and pulled me closer. His lips were on mine. His kiss was gentle and soft. I could feel his hold on me tighten as he lifted my body from the floor. I wasn't sure what was going on with me, but I couldn't fight him off, nor did I want to.

Pierre's mouth lowered down my body to my neck. I could feel his cock pressing against me through his trousers. Just the thought of having sex with this man was beginning to make me wet with desire. My body began to sway as he began moving toward my bedroom. I wanted to protest, but I didn't have the will. Kicking the door open with his foot, he entered my room and gently placed me on the bed. I must have passed out for a moment because when he called out to me, all of his clothes were off, and he was leaning over me. As much as I didn't want this to happen, I couldn't take my eyes off his gorgeous body.

Pierre swiped a stray hair from my face and began kissing me once again. It was like my body wasn't my own. "No, Pierre, I can't do this," I slurred.

"Shh... *Mon amour*, I know what you need," Pierre whispered.

Lifting my hips, Pierre slid my pants from my hips, down my body, and tossed them to the floor. With my bare skin exposed to him, he began placing kisses up my body to the top of my thighs. Just the feel of his lips on my skin was making my body burn with desire. When he got to my sex, he kissed me through the material of my lacy underwear before he slipped them off. Working his way up my body, he began unbuttoning my blouse. Cradling my body next to his, he slipped the soft fabric over my shoulders and down my arms. Still holding me close, he unfastened my bra and tossed it to the floor next to the rest of my discarded clothing. Something in my head was telling me this was wrong. His mouth moved to the valley between my breasts, where he began sucking and licking before moving on to my taut nipple. As he placed his mouth over the bud, my back arched into him, consuming his every touch.

I could feel the wetness between my legs rise as his words filled my head. "You are mine, *Mon amour*. One day you will realize that."

Unable to speak, I could feel him begin to push inside me. His movements were slow and tender. All I could think about was wanting more. I moved my hips to match his motion, and his movements increased. The enormity of his cock began to stretch me as he pumped deeper and deeper inside me. The pleasure he was giving me outweighed the pain of being stretched to accommodate him. I could no longer move. Pierre continued to thrust harder and deeper inside. I began feeling a prick on my shoulder, then another on my breast, and then again on my stomach, sending a surge through my body. My release took over and spilled from my body. I knew he had also reached his release when his penis began pulsating, spilling his seed inside me.

~****~

I could hear my cell phone ringing to the sound of Adele's 'Hello,' but only faintly. At first, I thought I might have been dreaming. Opening my eyes, my vision was blurry. Sitting up in my bed, my head began to throb like someone beat me with a hammer. I just wanted everything to be quiet. Stumbling from my bed, I headed to the kitchen, where I found my phone. Adele began singing again. Looking down at the screen, Peter's name appeared. As shitty as I felt, I was in no mood to talk to him. Silencing the ringer, I slowly made my way back to my bed. No sooner than I got under my covers, there was a pounding on the door. Taking my pillow, I covered my head with it, hoping that whoever it was would leave.

The pounding finally stopped a few minutes later. Thankful that it stopped, I removed my pillow from my head so I could at least breathe better, only to find Peter standing at the end of the bed with his arms crossed at his chest. I usually would have been pissed at him for coming into my home without an invite, but my body and head hurt so bad, I didn't have the strength to yell at him.

"Lilly, why haven't you answered my calls? I've been calling you all morning," he scolded me.

"I must not have heard my phone ring." I didn't know what else to tell him. I couldn't only remember bits and pieces after having takeout with Pierre.

Pushing myself from my bed the best I could, I attempted to get to the bathroom. I knew something was wrong the minute I heard Peter's voice.

"God, Lilly, what happened to you?"

Looking down at my naked body, I was more concerned about the state of my digestion than the bite marks along my neck, chest, and stomach. I felt like I was going to be sick. Placing my hand over my mouth, I ran to the bathroom just in time for my stomach to spill its contents. I could feel Peter behind me as he gently took hold of my hair to keep it away from the bile that was spilling inside the toilet. I wasn't sure what was happening to me, but I had never felt this shitty after drinking.

Helping me stand, Peter held me while turning on the water to the shower. I wasn't even sure if I could stand long enough even to take a shower. Peter must have noticed my queasiness because he began stripping off his clothing. Lifting me, he walked inside the shower. Carefully placing my feet on the shower floor, he adjusted the showerhead so that the warm water was spraying directly at me.

The whole time in the shower, Peter never let go of me. I knew it was a struggle for him, especially when he tried washing my hair. After we were finished, Peter helped me out by lifting me into his arms. He grabbed a towel and began drying me off. Even though I still felt like shit, I wasn't dead. The way his muscles flexed as he rubbed the water off my body made my insides come to life. God, he was gorgeous. Wrapping a towel around his waist, he took another towel and wrapped it around my hair. I didn't like being dependent on him, but with the way he was making me feel, I could get used to this attention.

Not only did Peter help me take a shower, but he also helped me brush my teeth and comb my hair. I could tell he was thoroughly enjoying my being helpless.

By the way, he was looking at me, he was done being the caregiver. Settling me back in bed, he demanded, "Do you mind telling me what happened?"

"I don't know, exactly. All I can remember was that Pierre came over to apologize for yesterday. I remember having dinner together. I don't remember much after that."

"Well, let me refresh your memory, Lilly," Peter said with anger, making me pull the covers tighter around my shoulders. "Your boyfriend didn't leave until early this morning. And by the looks of your body, he took you for one hell of a fuckin' ride with his cock."

"Get out!" I shouted, tears spilling from my eyes as I tried to piece together what really happened last night.

# CHAPTER SEVENTEEN
## *Peter*

After leaving Lilly's, I took a long ride on my Harley. It was the only way I could clear my mind. I thought I knew the girl I was falling in love with. Something happened last night between her and that motherfucker. I never saw so many bite marks on one body at one time. Even though they didn't break the skin, I could see that they were bad enough to cause bruising. I knew I had no room to talk. I've done my share of kinky stuff with women. That all changed when I met Lilly. It just didn't make sense that Lilly would allow something like this to happen to her. The last time we were together was the first time I had punished her. It was toned down compared to what I was capable of. When she said she enjoyed it, it did something to me. I should never have spanked her. I thought I was past all that, but somehow, she brought it back. That's why I need to keep my distance from her. I'm too dangerous for her. I could end up really hurting her.

I thought for sure the ride would clear my head, but the only thing it did was make me think about Lilly. Heading back to the city, I decided to stop at the shop and do a little research on Mr. Pierre Marchand. Even though I knew he had Lilly believing he was a good guy, I had my doubts. Something just didn't sit right about the whole rape thing, either.

Pulling up to the shop, I could see that Sly, Hawk, and Ash were around. I didn't know what I would do without my men. We all served together in Iraq and developed a bond that no one could ever break. All of us have had our share of bad luck. I think that's why we were so close. We were a family, nine brothers, willing to die for one another. That's how Jagged Edge Security started.

When I opened the door, Ash was cleaning the barrel of an AK-47, while Hawk and Sly played a game of pool. When I started the security company and asked my brothers to join me, I got their input on how they wanted it to run. I will never forget the stink Hawk gave about putting a pool table in the shop. He figured that since most of our time would be spent here, there might as well be something to do to occupy their time. He claimed it was therapeutic.

Walking up to Hawk and Sly, I asked, "So where are the rest of the guys?"

"Mike went to grab some food, Ryan and Josh had a family thing to do, and Lou is over at the YMCA teaching a class," Hawk replied.

"Well, since you guys are here, I'm going to need some help. I need to find out everything we can on a Pierre Marchand," I advised, clenching my jaw.

"What's so important about this guy?" Ash asked, blowing off the residue from the barrel of his assault rifle.

"He's fucking Lilly." I could tell by the look on their faces that they thought I was joking. Little did they know, I wanted this motherfucker out of her life for good. He was bad news. "I think he may have drugged her to get it done."

Three hours later, I had no more information about Pierre Marchand than before. My only hope was that the other guys were able to find out something. I was able to find out that he arrived in New York only a few days after Lilly and became a member of Maximum Capacity the day after

Lilly did. Knowing this didn't sit well with me. He had all the characteristics of a stalker, if there ever was one.

Ash walked into my office with a grin on his face. This could only mean that he found something useful. "I got some information, bro. Mr. Marchand has been a busy boy. It seems he recently rented an apartment across the street from Lilly. I also found out some other stuff regarding his past. Looks like the charge of rape against that girl he was with in college wasn't his only rodeo. There were two more incidents when he transferred to Oxford University. Two girls came forward to the dean of students about being sexually assaulted, but nothing ever came of it. Needless to say, the girls ended up dropping out."

"Give me his address," I demanded.

Leaving the shop, I hopped on my bike and headed to the city. Everything about this man smelled like shit. I wouldn't be surprised if he didn't slip something to Lilly before he fucked her, as I suspected. The more I thought about it, the more pissed off I got. I needed to concentrate on the road before I ended up as roadkill.

Getting off my bike, I looked up across the street and counted the floors to Lilly's condo and then the floors to Pierre's apartment. It didn't surprise me to find that his floor was in line with hers. Placing my helmet over the back seat rest, I headed inside his apartment building. It seemed pretty classy and expensive, but that didn't mean shit to me. This guy was a lowlife no matter where he lived.

Wouldn't you know it? Just the man I wanted to see. Stepping off the elevator in his fancy designer suit, his eyes met mine. Without hesitation, I cocked my fist back and planted it against his jaw. He didn't see it coming. Lifting his limp body by the lapel of his jacket, I pulled his head close to my lips. "If you ever touch or come near Lilly again, you're a dead man."

I left Mr. Marchand slumped on the floor and headed across the street to Lilly's. I didn't like how things were left this morning, and I needed to set things straight with her. Cop was stationed outside her door just like I requested. One thing about changing the locks on her door, I had my own set of keys. Allowing Lilly to open the door herself, I knocked a couple of times and waited for her to answer. The door opened, and she was still wearing the matching shirt and short pajama set I left her in. Even though she wasn't all made up, she was beautiful.

When her eyes met mine, I asked, "Can I come in?"

Without saying a word, she backed away from the door and headed to the kitchen. Closing the door behind me as I stepped in, I watched as she pulled a glass from the cupboard and filled it full of water. I could still see the bruises the bite marks left on her skin. Now I wished I had done more damage to Pierre than just punching him in the face.

Walking up to her, I took the empty glass from her hand and led her to the couch. Pushing lightly on her shoulders, I guided her down onto the couch. Taking a seat beside her, I wasn't sure how I would begin explaining the information we found out about Pierre.

"Lilly, I think Pierre drugged you. That's why you can't remember what happened," I explained.

The expression on her face said it all. "Drugged, why would you think he drugged me?"

"Because there are some things you don't know about him?"

"Like what things, Peter?" she asked softly.

"Like the fact that he lives right across the street from you, like the fact that his college love wasn't his only run-in with the law. Like the fact that the guy is obsessed with you," I began. "I care about you, Lilly. Please believe me about this guy. He's dangerous."

Her eyes were showing signs of concern. Lowering my head, I lifted her chin and placed my lips on hers. Consuming her warmth, I deepened my kiss by parting her soft lips with my tongue. She began to relax as I continued to play with her tongue. Needing to have her closer to me, I lifted her by the hips and gently pulled her onto my lap. I knew it was a matter of time before she would feel what she was doing to me. Her body began pressing closer to mine, and the kiss was becoming more frantic. As much as I wanted to take her at this very moment, I needed to know her feelings weren't because of something else.

Breaking the kiss and pulling away so I could see her face, I looked deep into her eyes and asked, "What is going on in that pretty little head of yours?"

"Please don't leave me." Her soft voice sounded with urgency as her eyes filled with tears.

"I won't leave you, Lilly," I reassured her, pulling her back to me.

As much as I hated seeing her this way, it was comforting to know that she needed me. I couldn't think about anything else but being here with her. Even though I knew it could be bad for her to be with me, I couldn't let her be hurt ever again, even if I might be the one to hurt her. If she ever found out who I truly was, it would rip her apart. I just needed to make sure that never happened.

~****~

For the next couple of days, I stayed with Lilly. As much as I loved being with her, she needed to get out. I kept telling her I wouldn't let anything bad happen to her. Finally, on the third day of being cooped up, she gave in. The first thing I did was give her a ride to the gallery. I decided it was better for us to take her car instead of giving her a ride on my bike. She didn't feel much like driving, so when she handed me the keys to her car, I accepted.

When we got to the gallery, I noticed that something was off. I told her to wait in the car and lock the doors while I went to check it out. Being the stubborn woman she was, Lilly protested, but I managed to convince her to let me check it out first. Leaning over, I kissed her on the lips and exited the car.

When I pulled into the alley, I noticed that the back door was open. This was what triggered my concern. Taking slow steps, trying to soften the sound of the gravel underneath my boots, I finally got to the door. Stepping inside, I looked back to the car, making sure Lilly obeyed me. Seeing Lilly looking out the back window, I gave her a hand signal to stay put. When she nodded confirmation, I proceeded down the narrow path made in the storage room. Whoever was inside the gallery was kind enough to turn the lights on so I could at least see where I was going. Searching the storage room, I tried to find something I could use to defend myself. I spotted a long metal bar and picked it up.

The door to the showroom floor was closed, so I knew I had to be careful when I opened it. Turning the knob, I carefully pulled the door towards me. It was then that I felt a hand grab my shoulder. I lifted the bar and turned, ready to defend myself. "Jesus fuck, Lilly. I told you to stay in the car."

"I got scared. It was taking too long," she said softly.

Putting my finger to my lips, I whispered, "You stay behind me. Clear?"

Lilly nodded as she took hold of my free arm. Opening the door further, the lights were on in the showroom. This seemed odd. If someone broke into the gallery, the lights wouldn't be on. Rounding the corner, something soft pressed against me, and I heard a crashing sound. Looking up, I saw the face of a woman scared to death. "Take whatever you want. Please don't hurt me."

"Brie, what are you doing here?" I heard Lilly ask.

"I thought I'd tidy up a bit before we opened," she stated, out of breath.

"You scared the shit out of us. Why did you leave the back door open?" Lilly questioned.

"Because it was easier than having to put the boxes down to open it," she said.

Lilly and I headed back to her office after helping Brie pick up the contents that had spilled from the box she dropped when I ran into her. Brie was Lilly's new neighbor that just recently moved into her building. Lilly hired her to be her assistant when she found out that Brie was struggling with money. For some reason, Lilly felt the need to let me know who she was. She must have thought I thought she was a thief.

It was nearing noon, and Lilly still had a couple of hours of work to do. I suggested getting some lunch while she finished up. I couldn't have been gone for more than half an hour. I thought for sure nothing would happen in that short a time. Taking the sandwiches I got for the three of us, I headed back to the gallery, only to find Lilly behind her desk with tears streaming from her eyes.

Setting our lunch on the coffee table, I walked to her and knelt in front of her. "Lilly, what's wrong? Did something happen?"

"Pierre was here," she said between breaths.

"Motherfucker! Did he hurt you?" I said, gritting my teeth.

"No. Is it true, Peter?" Lilly asked, moving her eyes to mine.

"Is what true, Lilly?" I asked.

"Was I adopted? Do you know my real mom?" she asked, looking deep into my eyes for the truth.

I wanted to tell her, 'No,' but I couldn't. Even though Lawrence and Kate Davis weren't her birth parents, they loved her more than anything. If it hadn't been for Rade and his need to protect Dylan, I wouldn't have found out. He had me check out every person Dylan was close to, including Lilly. Lilly had been adopted when she was very young. Her mother was a drug addict and DFS stepped in and took Lilly away from a bad situation. Lawrence and Kate adopted Lilly a year later when she was five. There was more to her childhood that I didn't share with Rade. I knew if I did, the truth about my past would come out as well, and I couldn't risk it, knowing how I felt about Lilly.

"Yes, I knew, Lilly. Rade requested a background check be done on everyone in Dylan's life," I said softly, unable to look at her tear-stricken eyes.

"Look at me, Peter," she said. "Why would you keep this from me?"

"I didn't think it was my place to tell you. Your mother wasn't a good person, Lilly," I began, rising to my feet. "She raised you on the streets and was addicted to drugs. You were awarded to the state. Even though the Davis' aren't your real parents, you're their daughter, Lilly, and they love you as if you were their own. You couldn't ask for better parents."

"I need to get out of here. Please take me home."

# CHAPTER EIGHTEEN
## *Lilly*

As much as I tried to, I couldn't stop the tears from falling. I felt like everything I knew about my life was based on a lie. I never expected the one man who hurt me the most was the one who told me the truth. I knew there was more to my past than what Peter was willing to tell me. Maybe this had to do with the secrets he was keeping from me. I knew I wasn't going to get them from him. The only other two people who knew about my past were my parents. Thankfully, they were still in Manhattan taking care of business.

Instead of calling them, I decided to head over to The Ritz and confront them personally. Hopefully, they would be ready to answer my questions. I wasn't leaving until they did.

I didn't say a word to Peter as he helped me out of the car. He must have taken the hint that I wanted to be left alone. Handing me my keys, he kissed my forehead and simply said, "Cop is at your place waiting for you. Call me later if you want."

Taking the keys from his hand, I headed up to my condo. Only I didn't make it there. Instead, I punched my floor and the third floor as well. I hoped it was enough to make Peter think someone got on at three while I got off at twelve. I knew I only had a short window before Cop would let Peter know that I didn't come to my condo. I needed to speak with my parents, which was the only way I knew I could do it without an escort.

Arriving at The Ritz, I pulled my car up to the valet parking area and waited for an attendant to assist me. Handing my keys to the valet, I headed inside the luxury hotel. When I got to the room my parents were staying in, I knocked gently on the door. I only had to wait a few seconds before my father answered the door.

"Lilly, this is an unexpected surprise," he said, moving aside so I could enter their suite.

"We need to talk. Where's Mom?" I asked, scanning the room.

"She should be here any minute. She's just finishing up at the spa," he said. "What is this about, sweetheart?"

"I'd rather explain when Mom gets here." I wanted both of them here when I confronted them about the truth they had been keeping from me for twenty years.

I took a seat on the couch while I waited for my mom to arrive. Dad had offered me something to drink, but I refused. I didn't know why I was so nervous about confronting them with the truth. I wasn't the one hiding things. I was jumpy, and my dad could tell I was getting anxious.

"Let me call down to the spa and see when she will be here," he said, walking over to the hotel phone.

The minute he picked up the receiver, the door to the suite opened, and my mother appeared. Closing the door, she turned to me with a smile of surprise.

"Lilly, sweetheart, what are you doing here?" she asked.

"I needed to talk to you both. You may want to sit down," I suggested. Once they were both seated, I began. "I want to know everything about the adoption and my real mother."

My dad looked at my mom with surprise. Somehow, I think he thought she might have been the one who told me. "Don't look at me that way, Lawrence. I didn't say anything to Lilly," she said.

Standing on my feet, I looked at both of them. "The information didn't come from either one of you. I just want to know the truth about my past."

My dad was now pacing the floor, drawing his hand through his thick gray hair. "We should have told you a long time ago. Please sit, Lilly, and I will tell you everything."

Taking a seat on the couch, I waited for him to explain.

"Your mother and I couldn't have children of our own, so we went through the process of adopting one. We always hoped to have a little girl, so when the adoption agency informed us that they knew of a little girl who needed a home, we became interested. You were only four at the time. We loved you the minute we saw you. About a year later, on your fifth birthday, we brought you home."

"What about my real mom? I want to know about her," I asked.

My dad took a seat next to me, as my mom moved closer to me on the other side. "They said that your mom was in a bad place. She was a drug addict. The lady from Family Services said your mom didn't even fight them when they took you away."

"Is she still alive?" I questioned.

"I don't know. We've never met her, nor have we ever heard from her," my mom chimed in.

"What is her name?" I asked hesitantly.

"Diana Walker," Dad said.

"Do you know if I have any brothers or sisters?" I asked, looking back and forth between them.

"You have a brother. He's a bit older than you. Other than him, there were no other siblings," he said, lowering his head.

"What happened to him?"

"I'm not sure. Something happened at the foster home he was at. They wouldn't tell us since we weren't family."

"What is his name?" I asked, feeling my eyes begin to water.

Taking me by the hand, my dad said, "Adam."

When I let The Ritz, my heart, was filled with sorrow. I had a brother, and I couldn't remember him. My mom and dad said they adopted me when I was five, but I couldn't remember anything before then. I couldn't even remember what my real mom looked like. I wondered if she was even still alive. I knew my dad and mom loved me, and it really shouldn't matter what happened in my past, but I really wanted to know.

~****~

Walking down the hall to my condo, I could see that Cop was talking to Brie outside her door. I could feel his eyes on me as I walked past them. "Hey Brie," I said, without acknowledging Cop. I took the keys from my bag, opened my door, and went inside before Cop could lay into me about disappearing. I'd had all the drama I could deal with for one day. Dropping my bag on the floor, I headed to the kitchen to pour myself a glass of wine. More than anything, I needed to sort out the information from the day. Sitting on my couch, I took my laptop from the table and placed it on my lap.

If what my parents said about my birth mother was true, I knew there had to be some information about her on the Internet. I pulled up the Internet and went to my favorite search engine. Typing in 'Diane Walker,' the search wheel began to spin. When the wheel stopped, the results appeared. I couldn't believe there were so many Diane Walkers in New York. Scrolling down the search hits, I found the one link that might give me the information I needed. 'Woman faces five to ten in drug bust.' Clicking on the link, I scrolled down to the story. 'A Homeless woman by the name of Diane Walker made a deal with the NYPD for information relating to a drug deal gone bad in Queens. According to Diane Walker, she was in the wrong place at the wrong time. Considering her state of mind, Ms. Walker's testimony is still under investigation. Having recently been stripped of her parental right by the state of New York, Walker was hesitant to cooperate. The names of her children have been withheld.'

Even though the article was twenty years old, at least it gave me something to go on. It was getting late, and my eyes were beginning to sting from the research I did on the Net. Closing down my laptop, I placed it back on the coffee table. Grabbing my bag, I searched for my phone as I walked to my room. There were six text messages from Peter asking me where I was and why I hadn't texted back or called. It was the last one that got me, though. *"Lilly, please call me or text me back. I need to know that you're okay. God, Lilly, please."* I lifted the phone to my ear and waited for him to answer. I figured the least I could do was let him know that I was okay.

"Lilly, thank God, you had me going fucking crazy," Peter blurted.

"I needed to talk to my parents," I said.

"Why didn't you let me know? Did they tell you what you needed to know?" he asked.

"Yeah, I'm tired, Peter. Can we talk tomorrow?"

"I'll be over in the morning. Sleep tight," he said before hanging up.

Throwing my phone on the bed, I walked to the bathroom to brush my teeth and got ready for bed. Finding my favorite pajamas, I slipped them on and crawled into bed. I thought for sure I would fall asleep as soon as my head hit the pillow, but my mind went into overdrive as I began thinking about everything that happened. Even though Peter knew about my real mom and kept it from me, I couldn't blame him for not wanting me to know the truth. I was the child of a drug addict. Who in their right mind would want to know that? Still, it was something that I needed to know about. There were so many things I wanted to know that only my real mom could answer. I wanted to know about my brother and what he was like. I wanted to know why she chose the life she did, still bringing me into her shitty world.

The more I thought about everything, the more it made me wonder how Pierre knew about my adoption and my past. Maybe Peter was right about Pierre. Maybe he was obsessed with me. He certainly made it his priority to find out about my past.

# CHAPTER NINETEEN
## *Lilly*

It was no surprise that I slept as late as I did. It was well after two in the morning by the time I finally fell asleep. Pushing from my bed, I headed to the bathroom to relieve myself and brush my teeth. As I was finishing up my duty, there was a knock at the front door. Pulling up my pajama bottoms, I hurried to the door. Just like he said, Peter was standing on the other side with a brown paper bag that I assumed was filled with bagels from the bakery down the street.

Grabbing the bag from him, I left him at the door and made my way to the kitchen. I set the bag on the counter while I grabbed two mugs from the cupboard; Peter was already by my side when I turned to fill the mugs. Placing his hands over my messy bun, he pulled out the hair tie and let my hair fall. The smile on his face told me what he wanted. Pushing him away, I said, "Food first, then sex."

I could tell he wasn't happy with my plan by the way his bottom lip curled over his top one. He was so cute when he pouted. Even so, I was starving. Taking my cup of java and the bag of bagels, I rounded the breakfast bar and took a seat. Pulling out the cream cheese and my favorite bagel, covered in cinnamon and sugar, I layered on the cream cheese. We sat in silence as I began devouring the delicious masterpiece I created.

By the time I had the last bite of my bagel down, I was stuffed. Leaning back in my chair, I padded my belly and confessed, "I am so full I could explode."

Peter must have interpreted my words differently, because he leaned over and whispered in my ear. "Play time."

Before I could protest, he lifted me from my seat and had me over his shoulder like a caveman. Slapping his back, I said, "Wait, Peter."

Stopping in his tracks, he said, "Oh no, you are not getting out of this."

I couldn't help but laugh. He always had a way of making me smile. It wasn't long before we were stripped out of our clothing and lying on my unmade bed. Taking my hands, Peter lifted them above my head and began kissing me. He stopped only to kiss the remaining bruising, which was now a yellow color mixed with green. I knew what Pierre did to me bothered him. Peter told me what he did to Pierre when he saw what happened to me. I didn't think violence was how to handle things, but Peter laying into him was justly deserved.

My thoughts were shaken when Peter's mouth clamped around my nipple. With a slight tug of my nipple between his teeth, my body was filled with a need only he could satisfy. As I struggled to be freed so I could wrap my arms around him, Peter's grip tightened around my wrists. "Peter, please. I need to touch you."

"Not yet, baby. It's all about control," he whispered.

Peter's mouth lowered further down my body. I could feel every muscle in my being stimulated as every soft wet kiss hit my body. I was on fire with desire for this man. Lowering his mouth further yet, his tongue was on my clit, making slow circular movements around the hard nub. It was driving me crazy not being able to touch him. When he slipped two of his fingers inside me, my willpower gave way. All of the tension I had been carrying dissipated as my orgasm took hold.

Peter waited until my body calmed before he released my hands and let me hold him. As he softly kissed me, my tears finally escaped. Peter placed gentle kisses over each eye as if to soothe my breakdown. "Shh... it's okay, baby. I'm here."

It was all I needed to hear. He was here. With me. Making love to me. The warmth of his hand slid down my body. Guiding his shaft to my entrance, he slowly entered me with no rush or demand. Only slow, tender movements were delivered as he eased his way deeper and deeper inside me. He knew my body and what I needed. Once again, my body shuddered as my release filled my body. His soon followed with three words of confession, "I love you."

~****~

We must have lain in bed for hours, just holding one another. I felt safe next to him. I knew Peter would never let anything bad happen to me. Lying next to him, listening to the beating of his heart, I knew he was the only person I could trust. I knew he was the only person I trusted to help me find my real mom. Taking in a deep breath, I pushed away from his body, propping myself onto my elbows. Looking down at him, I saw the man who just confessed his love for me. Swiping a stray hair from his forehead, I continued to stare at his beautiful face.

Startling me, he whispered, "The way you're looking at me, I get the impression you want to ask me something."

While his eyes were still closed, I lowered my hands and placed my chin on them, and asked, "How could you tell that I wanted to ask you something with your eyes closed?"

"That, baby," he began, flipping me over, so I was now on my back with him on top. "Is because I can feel it in your heartbeat, in your breath. So spill?"

"My mom and dad told me who my real mother was. I want you to help me find her," I asked nervously.

"Are you sure that's a good idea? What if you find something you wish you didn't? I know how these things turn out, Lilly. I don't want you to be disappointed or worse, hurt," Peter said.

"I have no choice, Peter. I needed to find answers. I need to know the truth about her and why she let me go so easily."

After two more bouts of sex and a mind-blowing blow job in the shower, Peter finally agreed to help me. With the connections he had, I knew he would be able to get the information I needed to find out if she was even still alive and where she might be living.

It was close to noon by the time we finished with our shower and left my condo. One thing that concerned me about Pierre: if he lived across the street, he would know when I left and when I came back. This made my heart beat faster, knowing that he knew my every move.

As we crossed the street to where Peter's Camaro was parked, I looked up at the apartment building, wondering if Pierre was watching us at this very moment. Peter must have felt my uneasiness. He squeezed my hand and said, "I know what you're thinking, Lilly. You don't need to worry about Pierre. He no longer lives across from you."

"Where does he live?" I asked as Peter opened the passenger door for me.

"You don't need to worry about that either. If he comes within fifty feet of you, I'll know," he reassured me, lowering his lips to mine.

I couldn't help but wonder what he meant by that unless he had one of his guys keep an eye on him. Buckling my seat belt, I took one last look at the tall building before Peter pulled away from the curb. It didn't matter what time of day it was. The traffic in Manhattan was close to unbearable. You wouldn't be able to tell by the way Peter effortlessly weaved in and out of it. Before long, we were out of the city and heading towards Queens. It was the first place I thought to look. Peter agreed with me after making a few phone calls while I got ready.

Most of the homeless people lived in Jackson Heights or East Elmhurst. We decide to start there. Hopefully, someone would be able to recognize her. She was only seventeen when she got pregnant with me, making her around forty-two or forty-three now. Even though I didn't have a picture of her, I guessed that she looked like an older version of me.

Hitting Queens, I began searching for homeless shelters in the Elmhurst and Jackson Heights area. There were so many of them. It was going to be like searching for a needle in a haystack. Peter suggested we check the older ones first. He said that most homeless people are creatures of habit. Once they are comfortable with their surroundings, they tend to avoid change. They don't trust people. They also tend to hold tight to their belongings. Belongings they would kill for.

Our trip to Queens was turning out to be a waste of time. We had been to at least a dozen homeless shelters. No one knew of Diana Walker. We were heading back to the car when an older man came up to us. There was no mistaking that he had been living on the streets for some time. He was wearing torn clothing and looked like he hadn't showered in months.

"You looking for Blondie?" the man asked.

"You know Diana Walker?" Peter replied.

"Yeah, I know her. Only everyone calls her Blondie. What do you want with her?" he sneered, spitting on the concrete.

"Do you know where we can find her?" Peter asked, walking closer to the older man.

"Depends," he said, holding his hand out like he was expecting something from us.

Peter pulled out his wallet and handed the older man a twenty-dollar bill. The man slowly reached for it and stuffed it in the pocket of his torn pants. Looking back at Peter, he said, "You may want to check the camp. That's where you'll most likely find her."

"Where is this camp?" Peter questioned the older man.

"It's in Weeping Beech Park. Ask for Termite. He can help you get to her," the old man instructed, throwing his backpack over his shoulder and walking away.

After talking to the homeless man, I felt like I needed to take a long shower. Even though I didn't get near him, letting Peter do all the talking, I felt like I needed to wash the stink off my body. Even though Peter didn't touch him either, I still pulled out my sanitizer and handed it to him. As he looked at me like I grew a new set of horns, I grabbed his hand and squirted a dab onto his palm. "Don't look at me that way, Peter. Who knows what kind of diseases he might have?"

The park the homeless man mentioned was only a couple of miles from where we were. Peter was trying to find a place to park while I looked around safely. Looking at the park, no one would be able to tell that a homeless camp resided inside. Parking the car, Peter and I got out and headed to the park's entrance. The deeper we got inside the park, the more we could see the homes of the homeless made out of cardboard and blankets. I took hold of Peter's hand, gripping it as if my life depended on it. A few homeless men were sitting on a park bench nearby. Peter approached them. There was no way I would trust these men, so I positioned my body behind Peter's.

"Excuse me," Peter said, watching one of the men looking straight at him. "I'm looking for a man named Termite."

"I'm Termite. What do you want?" an older black man asked.

"A friend of yours said you could help us find Diana Walker. She goes by the name of Blondie," Peter answered, pushing me further behind him.

"Yeah, I can take you to her, but it'll cost ya," he said.

Once again, Peter pulled his wallet from his back pocket and handed the man a twenty. When the man stood there without moving his hand, Peter knew he wanted more. After Peter placed another twenty in his hand, the man finally stuffed the money in a small bag hanging around his neck.

"Follow me," he said, leaving his friend on the bench.

I wasn't sure how long we had walked, but I was beginning to get the feeling that we had been taken. The only thing homeless people knew how to do was survive, even if it meant conning forty bucks out of us. I was about to tell Peter that I thought he'd been taken when the man stopped and pointed to a tent nestled between a couple of trees. The tent was made out of a large blue tarp, with rope to keep it in place. There was a piece of cardboard leaning against the front of the tent, which was used to keep out the cold.

As we walked closer to the tent, we could see that the tarp wasn't in the best shape. It looked to have been very well used, with several tears in it. Being who he was, Peter knocked lightly on the cardboard, careful not to knock it over. A loud voice came over from inside. "I don't want whatever you're selling,"

Peter looked over to me. I switched places with him, squatting in front of the tent. "We're looking for Diana Walker. Are you her?" I asked.

"Who wants to know?" the woman asked coldly.

"Her daughter," I said, looking up at Peter.

I could hear rustling inside the tent. I pushed back to standing and backed away from the ratty tent. When the cardboard fell forward, and the woman appeared, I saw myself. The woman had the same color eyes and hair like me. Her frame was smaller, but that could be due to the drugs and lack of food. The woman stood and focused her eyes on mine. In a soft voice, she said, "Lillabell."

# CHAPTER TWENTY
## *Peter*

The minute Lilly's mom looked at me, I knew she was deciding whether or not she knew me. It had been over fifteen years since she had seen me. I was just a young kid then, skinny and scrawny, but when I saw her standing behind a tree at the cemetery where Adam was buried, I knew who she was. When Lilly offered to take her to get a decent meal, I just about flipped. There was no way I would be able to get out of this. I just hoped we could get through the meal without her saying something.

We decided to take Lilly's mom to a small café just down the street from the park where she was living. We thought it would be better to start small. Lilly wasn't too sure how she would react to being around people. When we were seated, I could tell Lilly's mom wasn't as sheltered as Lilly thought. She might be able to fool Lilly, but she didn't fool me one bit. She knew exactly what she wanted and how to get it.

There was minimal conversation during our meal, which for me, was a good thing. It wasn't until Lilly excused herself to go the restroom that the real Diana Walker came out.

"I know who you are. I saw you at that cemetery. You may not look the same, but I knew it was you. Does Lilly know what you did to her brother?" Diana hissed as she pointed her finger at me.

"I was wondering when you were going to bring that up," I replied. "Whatever you think, Diana, what happened to your son was an accident."

"Hogwash. You may have been able to fool the authorities, but I know my son didn't just fall from that treehouse," she barked, picking at her food. "So here's the deal. You give me what I want, and your little secret stays between us."

Before I could find out what she really wanted, Lilly walked back to the table. Looking first at me and then her mom, she knew something was up. Taking her place next to me, she was about to say something, but her mom chimed in.

"So your boyfriend here has offered to help me find a new place to live, closer to you. Isn't that wonderful, Lillabell?" she proclaimed, looking right at me.

"Peter, is that true?" Lilly asked, confused.

"Yeah, I thought it would be good to have her closer to you," I lied. I wasn't sure what Diana's game was, but I knew I had to play along, at least for now.

Lilly wrapped her arms around my waist and laid her head on my shoulder. Looking over to Diana, I made an ultimatum of my own. "There's one condition that Diana has agreed to. She's agreed to stay clean and go to regular NA meetings," I declared with a grin.

After dinner, we headed back to the park. Diana wanted to grab her things that she had Termite keep an eye on. Knowing that she wasn't going to be living in the camp any longer, she didn't want to leave behind what few belongings she had. After she gathered all her things, we headed to the car. I popped the trunk and loaded the green garbage bag full of her shit into the trunk.

Once we were back in Manhattan, I located a motel with a reasonable rate for Diana to stay until I could find other living arrangements. Leaving Lilly and Diana in the car, I walked to the motel office to get her a room. When I got back, Lilly had tears in her eyes. I thought for sure Diana had broken our deal and told Lilly what happened to her brother.

Opening the door for her, I asked, "Are you okay, Lilly?"

Looking up at me, she answered softly, "Yeah."

I wasn't sure what else I could say without making things worse, especially if the cat was out of the bag. I took Lilly by the hand and helped her out of the car so Diana could slide out of the back seat. I handed Diana her room key and watched as they said their good-byes. It wasn't long before we were back in the car and on our way to Lilly's place.

With one hand on the steering wheel and the other holding Lilly's hand, I turned my head while still trying to keep an eye on the road. "Are you going to tell me why you were crying?"

"I asked my mom why she chose to live on the streets instead of fighting for me," Lilly said.

"And... what did she say?" I asked.

"She said she didn't have a choice. She said she ran away from home because she couldn't take the abuse anymore. She said my brother was the result of that abuse. Every time she looked at him, she remembered how he came into the world. That was when the drugs started. She needed something to block out the pain. She became addicted, but even the drugs couldn't help. So she decided to get rid of the problem. She left him at the fire station. He was four. A few years later, she became pregnant with me. She knew she needed to change her ways. She stayed clean until I was born. She was able to stay at a women's shelter with me since I was just a baby. It was getting harder for her to stay clean. The shelter found out that she was using again and call DFS. She got kicked out, and I was taken away from her after she was given several chances to get clean." Lilly's eyes began to fill with tears as she explained her mother's story.

I couldn't stand the torment she was going through. I pulled over the first chance I got and put the car into park.

Pulling Lilly towards me, I lifted her body over the center console, placing her on my lap. Her head cradled under my chin as her tears fell. "It will be okay, Lilly. Sometimes people make choices that aren't necessarily the right ones. I think your mom did what she could with what she had."

Lifting her chin, I brushed the last of her tears from her face and lowered my lips to hers. Her lips were soft and swollen. I could taste a hint of salt from the tears that had fallen. Lilly's arms wrapped around my shoulders as her breasts pushed against my chest. I could feel the onset of my arousal as the confines of my cock began to get tighter. As much as I hated it, I knew I needed to stop. The last thing I wanted was to be so far gone with desire that the world would see just how badly I needed her.

Breaking our kiss, I whispered. "Are you ready to go?"

Lilly pushed from my body with a slight nod and scooted over the console and back into the passenger seat. Once she buckled her seatbelt, I put the car into drive and pulled out of the parking lot. I caught myself looking over to Lilly several times during our drive, just to make sure she was okay. Even though she had fallen asleep, I still couldn't help but look at her. She was the most gorgeous woman I had ever seen. I just wanted to get her back to her place as quickly as possible so that I could alleviate the hard-on I had since we left that parking lot thirty minutes ago.

Fifteen minutes later, I pulled into the parking garage at Lilly's. She hadn't moved an inch in the last half an hour. This day had to have been hard on her. Getting out of the car quietly, I rounded the back and opened her door. Unbuckling her seat belt, I glided my hand under her thighs and lifted her carefully from the car. She didn't even stir, other than to nestle her head on my shoulder. Walking to the elevator, I could hear her soft moans, which was doing a number on my dick.

By the time we got to her condo, there wasn't an inch of space left where my raging hard-on was sitting, and my jeans were rubbing against the head of my cock. Placing her on her bed, I removed her shoes, took the blanket draped over her chair, and laid it over her body. God, how badly I wanted her. The minute she woke up, I would be getting my fill of her sweet tight pussy.

~****~

Lilly never woke up so I could get what I needed. The light shining through the window in her living room told me that it was morning. I must have fallen asleep sitting up because the back of my neck was stiff, and my feet were propped up on the coffee table. I could have kicked myself in the ass for not going to Lilly's room so I could be near her. Looking at my watch, I could see it was still early. Pushing up to my feet and stretching out the kinks in my neck and shoulders, I made my way to the kitchen to find some coffee.

I left the coffee brewing while I headed down the short hallway to check on her. When I got to her room, she was still sleeping. She must have gotten hot during the night because she was wearing only her panties and a t-shirt. Sliding next to her, I took in her warmth. I could hear her soft whimpers as I began kissing her behind her ear. God, this woman smelled good. Moving my arm over her body, I slowly lowered it under her frilly underwear. With my middle finger, I separated her slick folds and began teasing her.

Her body began to come alive as she rolled over onto her back to give me even better access. Slipping her pretty panties down her smooth legs, I nudged her legs wider as I positioned myself between her legs. Her back began to arch, signaling that she wanted more. Sliding my tongue through her wet folds, I lapped up her sweet juices, stopping at her perfect hard nub. Grabbing her ass, I pressed deeper into her soft skin while pulling her upwards until her hips were off the bed. Holding her there, I continued my assault on her sweet pussy. Kissing and sucking her clit, I could taste the beginning of her arousal. It took everything I had not to plunge deep inside her and feel her tight walls around my cock. Lilly's soft moans escaped as I slipped one, then two fingers inside her tight cunt. Finding the one spot that only a few men could, I began rotating my fingers while still devouring her swollen nub with my tongue. Her hips began gyrating against me, letting me know she was close. Freeing my fingers from the confines of her delectable pussy, I gathered more of her juices with my index finger and moved it lower to her back door. God, how I wanted to take her there. Eventually, I would. But for now, I just wanted to pleasure her.

Good and lubricated, I slowly worked my finger inside her tight pucker. Getting only to the first digit, I felt her body spasm with release, causing her rectum muscles to tighten around me. How badly I wanted it to be my cock buried deep inside her. With my cock throbbing, needing to be freed, I pulled off my jeans and hovered above her with my elbows resting on either side of her head. Kissing her softly on the lips, my cock found her entrance and submerged itself inside her like it had a mind of its own.

Unable to tame down my own desire, I lost my control and spilled my seed inside her. It was the most intense orgasm I had ever experienced. Spurt after spurt filled her. Fully emptied but not yet satisfied, I was ready for round two. Slow, and with gentle strokes, I moved in and out of her. Her body jolted once more as my own release took hold.

Diana was beginning to be the biggest pain in my ass. If I had been smart, I would have told Lilly everything. Only I didn't know how to tell her that I was the one who caused Adam Walker's death. I will never forget that day. It has haunted me every day of my life. Even at night, it creeps into my dreams. All I can see is him falling and the sight of his blood pooling around him. If he would have just left it alone and not pushed me the way he did, he would still be alive. I wouldn't have laid into him. I wouldn't have hit him. He wouldn't have fallen.

"Did you hear what I said?" Diana's voice rang through my cell, bringing me back.

"Yeah, I heard. Give me thirty minutes, and I'll be there," I said with gritted teeth.

I wasn't sure how much longer I could take her demands to keep her quiet. Having me take her shopping was the last straw. I wished I had never agreed to help Lilly find her. I should have gone with my gut and told her that her mother was dead. I could have easily made up some bogus story about her when she asked if I knew about her mom.

After I dropped Lilly off at the gallery, I headed to the motel where I had put Diana up. I needed to find a different place for her: some place safe, but inexpensive. Having other things on my mind, I missed the turn into the motel parking lot and ended up having to circle the block. As I was pulling into a parking spot, I noticed a poorly dressed man leaving Diana's room. Putting my car in park and I turned off the engine and headed in his direction. The closer I got to the guy, the better I could tell he was trouble. He was wearing a wife-beater, and the visible tats could only be the work of one man. Blade's signature artwork was on the man's arms and chest. Skulls and demon graphics lined his upper body.

Working in security, I have had my share of run-ins with drug dealers, and this guy had dealer written all over his face.

Blocking his way, I stopped him just shy of the stairs. Sizing him up, I took my chances, hoping he wouldn't be pulling a knife on me. I asked, "Mind telling me what business you have with Diana Walker?"

The guy must not have cared what I had to say because his hands pushed against my chest, throwing me off balance. With a slight stumble back, I kept my cool and asked him again, "I'm only going to say this once more. What business do you have with Diana Walker?"

The guy was ready to lay into me, but his reflexes weren't quick enough. I landed a punch across his jaw, causing him to stumble backward. Gaining his footing, he came after me again. This time he landed what I would call a powder puff blow to my cheek. Either this guy was a chump or stoned out of his mind. Just about to take another jab at me, I stopped his fist and twisted his arm so that it was now behind him. Leading him back to Diana's room, I knocked on her door.

"What did you forget, baby?" she asked, not realizing that I was standing at her door.

As she pulled her door open, a gasp of surprise left her mouth. "What the hell, Peter? Let him go."

"Not until you tell me what the fuck is going on and who this prick is!" I cursed.

"He's my boyfriend. Bud, meet Peter," she said, moving back from the door and allowing us to enter.

After visiting with Diana, I was more pissed off than before. It turned out her so-called boyfriend found out where she was, no thanks to her. He showed up to tell her he would do a construction job that would send them on their way to a better life. I knew that it was more than just a construction job he was trying to buffalo me with. He was into something a lot bigger, but it wasn't my job to find out. If I could be free of our arrangement, what did I care as long as she didn't say anything? It didn't surprise me when she pulled me aside.

"New deal," she began. "You give me a hundred bucks and let me stay here until Bud's job is finished, and I won't say a word to Lilly. I'll be out of your lives forever. You could tell her I was gone when you got here," she said.

"How do I know you won't come back or ask for more money?" I questioned, knowing how these things usually played out.

"Because Lilly is better off without me in her life. You and I both know that I can't give up the candy. Even though I know what you did to my son, I should be thanking you. I never wanted him in the first place, knowing how he came to be."

This was my lucky day. I pulled out five twenties from my wallet and handed them over. "I'll pay for your stay for two weeks, but after that, you're on your own."

Diana nodded in agreement. I think it was more than generous of me to flip the bill for her housing, knowing she had no intention of making things right with Lilly. I just hated to be the one to tell Lilly that Diana Walker wasn't the mother she needed.

## CHAPTER TWENTY-ONE
### *Lilly*

When Peter walked into the gallery, I knew something was wrong. I had expected him to spend a good portion of the day taking care of my mom. The look on his face said it all. Something happened. I knew I should have taken her instead, but I had an important meeting with an art dealer that I couldn't reschedule. I was finishing putting the final touches on a new display when he walked up behind me.

"We need to talk, Lilly," he said.

Looking up at him and getting the feeling that something bad happened, I asked, "What's going on, Peter? Did something happen to my mom?"

"She's gone, Lilly," he said, placing his hand on my cheek.

"What do you mean she's gone?" I asked, feeling pressure building in my chest.

"All I know is that when I got to the motel, the manager said she took off," Peter declared.

"We have to find her, Peter. She needs help," I said frantically. I knew that if she left, it was because she was going to go back to her old life. I didn't want that for her.

"Lilly, did you ever stop to think that maybe she doesn't want help? The life she's led is the only life she knows."

I knew Peter was right. She had led that life for so long, she probably didn't know any other way of living. An everyday life with a job and a decent roof over her head was probably foreign to her. I found out what I needed to know about her and why she chose not to fight for me. I may have lost her, but there was still a chance that my brother was still out there. I needed to focus on finding him. I knew she dropped him off at a fire station. Certainly, there had to be some information on him.

~****~

I should have been more focused on the meeting with the art dealer, but the only thing I could think about was trying to locate my brother. I caught myself several times pretending like I knew what the dealer was asking only to find I left him more confused. Even though it wasn't one of my more productive meetings, I did manage to sell two pieces of art to him. Glad that the day was almost over, I went to my computer, deciding to search for information on my brother. I typed in various keywords hoping to get a hit. My efforts turned up no hits until I typed in 'baby boy left at fire station.' That got a hit.

Reading the article, the story matched the explanation that my mom gave me. It stated that the little boy was examined by a pediatrician, deemed healthy, and appeared not to have been abused. It made me thankful that my mom was smart enough to take care of my brother by making sure he was fed and taken care of. As I read further down the article, I found out he had been taken to a children's shelter by the state until he could be placed in foster care. At least I knew where to start.

It was still early enough in the day that I decided to check out the shelter to see if anyone remembered him being brought in, but first, I needed to go back to my place to grab my car. Somehow I needed to get past Josh, who was watching the gallery from across the street. Heading to the back of the gallery, I grabbed a silk scarf that I had used for one of my displays and wrapped it around my head. Going out the exit door, I walked down the alley until the street was in view. Josh was in his car, watching the front door of the gallery. With his eyes directed at the entrance, I headed in the opposite direction, where I then hailed a cab to my building to get my car.

The shelter for children in the article was located in Brooklyn. Getting into my car, I punched in the address on my GPS and headed out of the parking garage. I knew Peter wouldn't be happy if he found out that I left without telling him, but I knew this was something I had to do alone.

Reaching the shelter, I thought about what my mom said. I had to be careful about what I said. I didn't want to get her in trouble for leaving my brother on the steps of the fire station. Even though there was a safe haven law in New York, I'm sure it didn't apply to my mom since Adam was more than 30 days old when she dropped him off.

Pretending I was a student writing an article about abandoned babies, I approached the older lady behind the front desk. I told her I was writing a story regarding pregnancy and young mothers unable to care for their babies and, therefore, the mother's had to abandon them. I was lucky to find that the older lady remembered the incident. She had been working at the time and remembered my brother. She remembered how cute he was and wondering how he could have been left at the fire station. The older lady mentioned that he had stayed at the shelter until he was about six, and then he was placed in a foster home.

The older lady was kind enough to give me the address where he was taken. She didn't have any other information on him since she didn't follow up with the foster home once he left the shelter. She was pretty confident that they would remember him, or at least have records of his stay, even though it was more than twenty years ago.

Three hours later, I was on my way back to my condo. Exiting the elevator, I turned the corner heading to my condo when I spotted Cop standing outside the door. His arms were crossed, and he had a look of annoyance on his face. As I walked up to my door, getting ready to pull my keys out, he took hold of the doorknob and turned it. Looking down at me, he said, "Good luck," as he pushed the door open.

Peter was sitting on the couch with a beer in his hand, looking like he was about to come unhinged. Placing my things on the breakfast bar, I looked toward him, knowing he was going to lay into me. "You don't have to say anything, Peter."

"Evidently I do, because somehow you just don't get it," he argued, standing while crossing his arms. "Lilly, you can't just take off and not let someone know where you're going, especially when we don't know what Pierre's next move is going to be."

"Peter, nothing happened, and you have eyes on Pierre," I said. "Besides, I had something that I needed to take care of."

"What was so important that you had to go alone, Lilly?" he asked.

"I went to find out about my brother. I know my mom is a lost cause, but maybe it's different for my brother. I need to find him," I confessed.

"I just don't want anything to happen to you. Promise me you won't take off without having someone with you," Peter demanded. "Were you able to find anything out?"

"Not really. I found the shelter where he was taken after my mom dropped him off. I want to check out the foster home he went to tomorrow. The lady at the shelter said he was sent there when he turned six. For now, I just want to take a long hot bath and go to bed."

Peter was within feet of where I was standing in seconds. Grabbing me around the waist, he pulled my body close to his. It wasn't long before his lips were on mine, and his tongue slid between them. I could feel the arousal under his jeans as he bent his legs and lifted me from the floor. My legs automatically wrapped around his waist. With his hands on my ass and mine wrapped tightly around his neck, he walked us to my bedroom, never breaking our kiss. Our bodies were pressed so close to each other, I could feel the beating of his heart sync with the beat of mine. Placing me gently on the bed, he slowly removed my slacks while keeping his lips on mine. My hands weaved through his thick hair, feeling the need to consume him.

With my slacks off, his hand began working their way up my body. Resting his hand softly on my breast, he began kneading the sensitive skin. I could feel the wetness beginning to pool between my legs. Struggling to get more of him, I lowered my hands between us and unfastened his belt. Freeing him of his jeans, the hardness of his cock pushed against my mound, making my body ignite with fever. Breathlessly, I moaned, "Peter." Feeling the warmth of his cock enter me, a surge of desire pulsated inside me, making me aware that the first onset of my orgasm was about to unfold. Pulling him closer, I planted my mouth on his and frantically pushed my tongue between his lips.

He broke the kiss and whispered softly, "Do you trust me, Lilly?"

I didn't know where he was going, but I trusted him completely. "Yes," I moaned, lowering my mouth to his neck.

His body was off of mine, and the feeling of abandonment filled my mind. Pushing up to my elbows, I watch as he pulled a tiny object from his pocket. It looked to be round and riveted with a ring on the end. Whatever he had in his hand, he laid it on the bed and flipped my body over. His fingers were between my folds, lapping up the juices I knew were thick between them. As he circled my tight pucker, I had a pretty good idea of what he was about to do.

Looking behind me, I watched as he slowly inserted the device in my butt. I clamped down on the invasion and bit down on my lip. "Relax, baby," he said, taking hold of my hip with one hand as he guided the butt plug inside me with the other.

Relaxing, I could feel the plug ease deeper inside me. The pain subsided, and there was only the feel of pressure taking hold. When it was fully lodged inside me, Peter leaned over me and kissed the small of my back. Releasing his hand from my hip, he trailed it up my body until I could feel the warmth of his fingers on my hard nipple. A slight pull on my nipple caused me to jump, making my muscles clamp down on the plug. My body was on fire. I could feel the tingling from head to toe. I felt the need to be satisfied. Peter must have sensed my angst because his cock filled me. The tightness was more than my body could take. I screamed with uncontrollable pleasure, unable to hold back my release.

Thrusting deeper inside me, the pulsating of his cock echoed yet another orgasm as his eruption filled me.

~****~

Lying in Peter's arms, something inside me was changing. I only knew this feeling once. I promised myself that I would never allow a man near my heart, only to have it torn in two. The problem was Peter was like no other man I ever knew. Yes, he had secrets, but he also did things to me that I had never felt before. The things he had done to my body, I thought I would never let happen, or enjoy for that matter. He made me want to give myself over to him and allow him to command my body. He asked me last night if I trusted him. I did, but only with my body. He was the only man who had ever told me that he loved me. I couldn't let my guard down and believe that those three words could possibly mean something.

Lost in my thoughts, I heard the faint sound of a vibration, which sounded like a cell phone. Pushing up to my feet, I knew it wasn't my phone vibrating, which only meant it had to be Peter's. Sifting through the discarded clothing on the floor, I found his phone beneath his jeans. Turning on his phone, I could see that a password was needed to access the full text. Seeing what I did of the text, I knew something was up. The words, 'It's done' appeared across the screen. I wished I knew what his password was so that I could read the rest of the text. Hearing him stir behind me, I turned to see his smiling face. "Come back to bed, baby," he ordered, patting the spot next to him.

Turning towards him, I crawled up onto the bed, holding his cell in my hand. "Someone was trying to reach you," I said naïvely, handing his phone to him.

Taking his cell from me, he placed it on the nightstand and proceeded to pull me closer to him. "Aren't you going to see who it was?" I asked.

"It's the middle of the night, Lilly. Whoever it is can wait till morning."

Maybe he could wait, but I couldn't. "What if it's important?" I said.

"If it will make you happy," he griped, turning his body to pick up his cell.

I tried seeing the password he entered on his phone, but he was too quick. Nuzzling closer to him, I try to get a better look at his screen to read the complete text. Either he was a speed reader, or he knew exactly what the text was about. Shutting down the phone, he placed it back on the nightstand and cuddled in close to me. "It's nothing," he said, kissing the top of my head before he closed his eyes once again.

~****~

The morning came too quickly. The only thing I could think about was the text that came in on Peter's phone. The only way I was going to find out what it was about was to ask him point-blank. Rolling over, I began kissing his muscular chest, hoping that I would be able to stir him awake. I could feel the beating of his heart increase and his breathing becoming quicker. Taking his warm taut nipple in my mouth, I began caressing it lightly with my tongue. I could hear a soft groan escape his mouth. Gazing up, I met with his beautiful smile. He pulled me up from under my arms and lifted me so that I was straddling him just below the magnificent 'V' of his waist.

Placing my hand across his hard chest, I asked innocently, "So what was the text about at three a.m.?"

"Nothing you need to worry about," he said, grazing his hand under my t-shirt.

"This is what I'm talking about, Peter. This is why we can never be together. I'm tired of the secrets," I blurted, pushing off his body.

Before I could get too far, he pulled me back to him. "It was work. My services are requested in Washington. Some international diplomat is flying in, and they need protection for him, so they contacted me."

"Why do they need you? Doesn't this guy have his own security?" I asked, not buying his story.

"Yeah, but they don't trust this guy," he said.

"Sounds kind of like an excuse not to tell me the real story." Pushing off the bed, I looked over my shoulder and said, "Did you want to join me?"

Peter flew so quickly off the bed, I thought he was going to trample me. Slinging me over his shoulder, he swatted my ass playfully. "Hey," I scolded him, slapping him on his tight ass as well. I could already feel the wetness building between my legs. I wanted nothing more than to feel him deep inside me.

Setting me down on the counter, he began searching the drawers. Knowing what he was looking for, I reached in front of him, pulled out the last drawer, and gave him an unopened toothbrush. Hopping off the counter, I found my own brush. Placing a dab of toothpaste on it, I began brushing my teeth. Rinsing out my mouth, I pretended like I didn't notice the way he was looking at me. I removed my t-shirt and walked over to the shower. Opening the glass door, I turn the handle to the hottest temperature, then closed the door and watched as the steam began to gather on the glass. Turning around to grab a towel, I caught Peter gawking at me. "What?" I asked cunningly.

"God, you're beautiful," he said softly, sweeping his hand across my lips before he lowered his to mine.

Pulling him closer to me, I tugged him into the shower under the hot spray. His shoulders pressed together as he tried to adjust to the temperature of the water. Soon his body relaxed as it got used to the hot water. Peter reached for my pretty pink loofah and squeezed a healthy amount of my favorite body wash in the center. Working the soap into a lather, he began sliding the sponge down my body, taking extra special care around my breast area. With the sponge on one side and his hand on the other, I could feel my nipples beginning to harden from his touch.

He knew exactly what he was doing to me. He placed the loofah under the hot water, soaking up more, only to end up squeezing the excess water so that it trailed down my body. The heat of the water had my body on fire. I spread my legs wider as Peter began trailing his hand down my stomach, down the apex of my mound until the rough texture of the sponge rubbed against my hard nub. The sensation was unlike anything I had felt before. Spinning me around, Peter shifted the sponge to the other hand and began using his free hand to separate the skin of my slick folds.

The sponge dropped to the shower floor, allowing Peter to begin tweaking the taut peaks of my nipple. My head fell back against his shoulder as my body absorbed everything he was giving. As he slipped not one, but two fingers inside me, I felt the friction begin to consume me, causing my body to jolt against his. The more I pushed against him, the more I felt the hardness of his cock on my backside, leaving me wanting even more of him.

Peter removed his fingers and placed his hands on my hips. "Place your hands on the wall baby," he ordered, breathlessly.

I did as he asked without hesitation. He lifted me, causing my legs to wrap around his hips. I arched my back and locked them at my ankles. I could feel the pressure of his cock at the ridge of my soaked entrance. What was he waiting for? I needed him inside me, but he was only moving enough to rub his cock between my folds. I could feel the beat of my heart getting faster. All I wanted was the feel of him inside. Then it happened. Euphoria. He slid inside me with such force that I swore my scream of pleasure was going to shatter the shower door.

Peter pulled me even closer to him, causing my hands to leave the shower's tile wall. Wrapping them around his neck for support, I felt his cock move deeper inside me. Peter had all the power as he lifted my body over and over again so he could pump further and further inside my channel. When I thought I couldn't take anymore, my body shattered with one orgasm after another.

Peter lowered my body while still holding me close. I wasn't sure if I could stand even if I wanted to. Holding me against him, he placed his lips on mine, kissing me with such passion, I knew I was in trouble. I was beginning to fall for him. There was no denying what my heart was saying. Soon I would be his.

# CHAPTER TWENTY-TWO
## *Peter*

When Lilly told me that she had been out looking for her brother, I just about lost it. I couldn't let her know what I was really afraid of, losing her. Her explanation of the events made me think about what could have happened if she found out the truth. I needed to get in touch with someone who could keep what really happened at the foster home away from her. If she ever found out the truth, I knew she would never forgive me. I also knew I would lose her forever.

Getting in touch with my friend at the Department of Family Services, I explained my situation to him. At first, he wasn't willing to help me, but then I reminded him of what I did for him and how he got a job working with children. Matt and I grew up on the streets together. Shortly after I came back to the States from my tour of duty overseas, I ran into him. He'd gotten himself into trouble and needed a friend more than anything. He was lucky that I was in the States and was able to provide him with an alibi. I knew there was no way he could have robbed that jewelry store. His story was that he heard the alarm go off as he was walking home from work. The stupid shit decided to investigate and walked right inside the store. The cops were on him in minutes. He looked guilty as hell, so they arrested him on the spot. I covered for him and told the cops that I was with him the exact time the alarm went off. The cops believed me since I was a hero. Later, I found out that even though Matt didn't break in, he stole some high quality diamonds that the thieves must have dropped when they left. He hid them in a safe place minutes before he was arrested. I never told anyone, and Matt put himself through college because of it.

Needless to say, he was able to pull a couple of strings to make sure Lilly wouldn't be able to tie me to her brother and his death. As far as Lilly was concerned, the text I had received was for a job in Washington. I wasn't lying about the job. I had been notified yesterday that I was needed to protect some crooked diplomat until he could testify against some well-known arms dealer. I was scheduled to head out later tonight. I really didn't want to leave Lilly behind with everything going on, but the money was too good to pass up even though it would be dangerous.

As much as I wanted to go with Lilly to the foster home where I spent the majority of my childhood, I couldn't risk someone recognizing me. Instead, I requested that Cop go with her. Vince "Cop" Coppoletti was one of the best men I had. No matter where he was or what he was doing, he never complained about having to drop everything to do a job for me. I could always depend on him.

Going through my emails, I waited for Lilly to finish getting ready. As she appeared before me just as I was finishing up, I couldn't take my eyes off her. Never has a woman made my dick as hard as it was at that very moment. Getting up from the couch, I walked over to where she was standing. Reaching behind her, I wrapped my arms around her waist, taking in the fruity scent of her perfume. God, how I wished I could capture her scent and take it with me to Washington.

Lilly's head tipped back and rested on my shoulder. Twisting her body so that she was facing me, I captured her lips with mine, giving her one last kiss before I headed out. I tangled my tongue with hers, feeling the warmth of her mouth taking me in. Deepening the kiss, I heard a soft moan, sending a rush of heat down my body to my throbbing dick. I wanted nothing more than to have one more round of sex with her. I knew that if I didn't get out of there right away, I would lose control.

"I need to take off, baby. Cop will take you to the foster home when you're ready." I softly kissed her on the head, leaving my body aching for more.

~****~

I never thought leaving Lilly would be so hard. I wasn't sure if it was because of the shit I was leaving behind or the fact that I already missed her soft body next to mine. Sitting at the airport waiting for my flight only made me think about Lilly and the danger I might be putting her in. This is why all of my relationships ended up in one-night stands. With the life that I led, I couldn't chance getting involved with anyone, but that didn't mean I couldn't satisfy my needs. With Lilly, it was different. Never before had I wanted a woman as much as I wanted her. Confessing my love for her was probably not the wisest thing I had ever done. She had a spell over me that I just couldn't break.

I hated flying. I was glad that at least I was seated in first class. It was the only way I would fly. As I took my seat, the flight attendant was there to take my drink order. I ordered a double Scotch, since I wasn't too keen on flying in the first place. It was the only way to tame down my fear of flying. I preferred to drive or ride my bike whenever I needed to be somewhere.

It was a six-hour flight to Washington, and unbearable, to say the least. The minute we landed, I was one of the first people off the plane. I hauled ass through the gate to baggage claim. I wanted to get out of this airport as fast as possible and into my hotel room. As I waited for my luggage, I quickly called Cop to see how everything was going with Lilly. Even though it was early, I needed to know how things went after I left yesterday morning.

"Cop, give me an update," I said, leaning against a pole as I watched the carousel spit out luggage from our flight.

"Not too much to report. I took Lilly to the foster home in Brooklyn. She didn't say much when she left. She looked disappointed that she didn't get the information she wanted. I dropped her off at the gallery after that," he explained.

"Where are you now?" I asked, hoping he would be at Lilly's place.

"Just getting ready to take a shower and grab some shut-eye. Josh is keeping an eye on her until I get back," he advised.

"I may not be able to contact you for a couple of days. If anything comes up, text me," I said.

"Will do."

At least I didn't have to worry about Lilly finding out anything. The way it sounded, she didn't find the information she was looking for. I just hoped that she would give up on finding her brother instead of continuing her search for answers.

~****~

The first thing I did when I got to my hotel was crash on my bed. I didn't even bother taking off my clothes. The tension of the flight left my body exhausted, and my nerves completely shot. It was no surprise I was out the minute my head hit the pillow. Then it began: the dreams. I hadn't had one of these dreams in a long time. Visions of Adam's face crept in. Over and over, I kept seeing the look in his eyes as my mind kept rewinding what I did. Everyone kept telling me it wasn't my fault. There was no way I could've held on to him. He was one-hundred ninety pounds to my one-hundred ten. I never told anyone what really happened. Instead, I lied and said he slipped, and I tried to pull him up, but I couldn't hold him. I was so angry with him. He kept telling me I was the son of a whore and that my mom fucked anything with a dick. He kept saying that my mom threw me away because it was the only way she could make money.

I should have never pushed him. I should have tried harder to pull him up instead of watching him fall. I hated him for what he said. My mother didn't leave me. She overdosed on whatever drug she was using. I remembered shaking her to wake her up. She never did. I always stayed near her. Kept her warm. Nothing helped. When the pounding on the apartment door began with the yelling, "I know you're in there, bitch. Where's my money, you fucking cunt?" I tried blocking it out by putting my hands over my ears. Eventually, the banging stopped, but I knew they would be back. They always came back. Only the last time, it wasn't them.

"Stop! Stop! Please don't take me away from my mommy," I yelled out. I tried to forget. It was always the same. First his eyes, then my mom's. Shaking my head to clear out the demons, I pushed myself from the bed and headed to the bathroom for a much-needed shower. Lathering my body with soap, I tried to picture something other than the thought of my nightmare. I tried to focus on the only person who could make me happy, the only person who could tame the demons. Looking down, I could see the erection that was surging between my legs. Gripping my shaft, I imagined Lilly's lips wrapped around me, stroking my dick with her warm mouth. I could feel the tip of her tongue tease the head of my cock while she sucked, pulling me deeper inside. My movements began to increase, seeing only Lilly's head move up and down as I thrust deeper and deeper inside her sweet mouth. My head fell back as I moaned, "Fuck," wishing she was with me now as I came with needed fury, covering the shower wall with my release.

After my scene in the shower, it was hard for me to concentrate on anything but Lilly, which only led to another hard-on. I needed to hear her voice. Taking my cell from the nightstand, I dialed her number and waited for her to answer.

"Hello," she said.

"Hey, baby. I just needed to hear your voice," I said like a love-struck teenager. "How did things go at the foster home?"

"Good, I guess. I found out that my brother died when he was fifteen. He fell from the treehouse they used to have in the back yard at the foster home. The person I talked to didn't know much about it other than some older boy tried to save him."

"Did they say anything about the older boy?" I asked, hesitantly.

"No. They didn't have any information on him. The couple that ran the home when it happened was no longer around, and they didn't have any information on where they went."

"I'm sorry, baby. At least you know what happened to him," I said.

"Yeah, I just wished I knew more about him and what he was like," Lilly said softly. "I found out where he was buried. I'm going to visit the cemetery this afternoon."

"Be sure that Cop goes with you," I ordered.

"Okay," she replied softly.

Everything in my heart told me I needed to tell her the truth about her brother. I just couldn't, though. As much as it pained me to hear the sadness in her voice, I knew it would kill her if I told her what really happened. I only wished I were there to comfort her.

## CHAPTER TWENTY-THREE
### *Lilly*

After talking with Peter, I was beginning to miss him more and more. It had been less than twenty-four hours since I had seen him, but my body was starting to have "Peter withdrawal" symptoms. I couldn't even concentrate at work without thinking about him. Brie was scheduled to come in at 1:00 p.m., which only gave me a couple of hours to get done what I needed before I left for the Peaceful Grove Cemetery, where my brother was buried.

Staring at my computer, I began to think about my real mom. It occurred to me that she didn't know that he was dead. As far as she knew, he was still alive, leading his own life. I wasn't even sure how to get in touch with her. Thinking about what Peter said about her just taking off, I decided to check with the manager at the motel she was staying at first. Hopefully, there was a chance she may have left information as to where she was headed in case someone came looking for her.

Once Brie arrived, it didn't take me long to gather my things and head out. Cop was already waiting for me. As he helped me get into his truck, I tried to get in as gracefully as possible without showing too much of my backside since I was wearing a skirt. I wished I had suggested he drive my car instead of his F250. I settled in the seat as he rounded the front and got in. Fastening my seatbelt, I looked over to him. "Can we make a quick pit stop before we head to the cemetery?"

"Not a problem. Where do you want me to take you?" Cop asked, easing his truck from the curb.

"I want to go to the motel where my mom was staying," I said.

Cop looked over to me with one of those looks that I recognized right away. It was the same look Peter gave me when he was trying to hide something. "Do you have a problem with that?" I asked, trying to gauge his reaction.

"No, ma'am," he said.

The minute Cop put the truck into park, I was out and on my way across the parking lot of the motel to the main office. I didn't care that my skirt slid up my legs, revealing the strap of the garter holding up my silk stockings. Before I could close the door to the truck, Cop was beside me.

"I think it would be better if you waited in the truck while I talked to the motel manager," he said sternly.

"Don't be silly. This will only take a minute. Nothing is going to happen to me between now and then," I said, noticing the uneasiness in his voice.

"I really need to insist, Lilly," he said forcefully, as he stepped in front of me, blocking my view of the office.

"What is this about, Cop?" I asked, beginning to feel the onset of anger approaching.

Looking over his shoulder, I couldn't believe what I was seeing. My mom was walking up the steps to her room. She hadn't left. She was still here. Pushing Cop aside, I headed towards her.

"Wait, Lilly," Cop said behind me.

Turning my body, I gave him one of my signature "piss off" looks. By the time I reached the stairs, my mom was already in her room. Climbing the steps as quickly as I could in four-inch heels, I could only think about how pissed I was that Peter lied to me. From where I was standing, I could see Cop, who was now pacing the length of his truck with his hands raking through his thick brown hair. He knew he'd been caught. He was just as guilty as Peter, as far as I was concerned.

Reaching my mom's room, I knocked lightly on the door. When she didn't answer, I yelled, "I know you're in there, Mom. Open the door."

When the door opened, I saw the face of a woman who had no intention of putting her life back together. Her pupils were the size of marbles, and her face was flushed. Pushing past her, I entered her room only to find a piece of aluminum in the shape of a spoon with a candle sitting beside it. Whatever was inside was gone. There was only a light brown residue left on the bottom.

"I thought you left?" I asked coldly.

"You aren't supposed to be here, Lillabell. That man of yours was supposed to convince you that I left," she said. "I told him I would keep my mouth shut."

"What are you talking about?" I questioned her, confused.

"Your brother and how he really died."

"You know about that?"

"Yeah, and so does your boyfriend. After all, he was there."

I wasn't sure if I could believe what I was hearing. She was so strung out on drugs, she wasn't making any sense. "You aren't making any sense."

I watched with confusion as she walked to the nightstand, grabbed the pack of cigarettes, and took one out. With shaky hands, she lit the cigarette and took in a deep breath. "Your boyfriend, that Peter fella, he was there when Adam died. They said your brother slipped and fell from that tree house and that Peter couldn't pull him up. Lies, all lies," she hissed, puffing her cigarette.

"What do you mean, Peter was there?" I asked.

"Ask your boyfriend. I've already said too much."

I watched with disbelief as she headed to the bathroom and closed the door. I couldn't believe that Peter would know Adam. How could he? I mean, what were the chances? Even though I didn't know about Peter's childhood, I knew he was a good person. Yes, he had his secrets, but this, this couldn't be true.

Leaving her room, I headed back to the truck where Cop was standing. My emotions were all over the place. Cop knew something was up. Looking him straight in the eye, I asked, "Did you know she was still here?"

Shaking his head and looking off to his right, unable to face me, he nodded, saying, "Yeah."

~****~

The ride to Peaceful Groves Cemetery was the longest ride I had ever taken in silence. I was so angry with Peter for lying to me that I didn't have any words to share with Cop. I knew Cop was only doing his job, but he should have said something the minute I asked him to take me to the motel.

I had no idea where my brother was buried, so I had Cop pull up to the groundskeeper's office to see if someone could let me know. The groundskeeper handed me a map of the cemetery and showed me where my brother was buried. He said that it wouldn't be hard to find since it was the only plot in that section that didn't have a headstone.

Cop pulled around to the north side of the cemetery to section 'G.' I opened the door and got out of the truck holding on to my skirt as I slid off the seat. Just like the groundskeeper said, there was no headstone where my brother was laid to rest. It made me sad to see that the only marker to show who was buried there was a small piece of metal with his name, Adam Lee Walker, with the date he was born and the date he died. Kneeling before the plate, I brushed my hand across it. "I'm so sorry that I didn't get a chance to know you, big brother. I bet you would have been the best."

It was beginning to get dark. Cop came up behind me and placed his hand on my shoulder. When I looked up at him, I knew it was time to go. Being in a cemetery after dark was probably not a very good idea. Pushing myself to my feet, I said goodbye to my brother, promising him that people would know who he was. Before leaving for the city, I had Cop stop at the shop across the street that made headstones for the cemetery. I wanted my brother to have more than just a piece of metal embedded in the ground. I wanted everyone to know who he was. By the time I left, Adam had a new headstone made of gray granite. Written on the front were the words, *"He lies in peace with no more sorrow, dearly missed always, today and tomorrow."*

~****~

When we got back to the condo, Cop took his place outside my door with no word. After thinking about what Diana said on the way home, I had to find out if it was actually true. Certainly, there would have been something said about it. Changing into my most comfortable pajamas, I poured myself a glass of wine and headed back to my room with my laptop. I had a pretty good idea of the time frame I needed to search for since the date Adam passed away was on the plaque where he was buried. I typed in several keywords to see if anything would come up. I got several links on the first try. Evidently, the death of a child was pretty big news back then. Clicking on the link, a picture appeared of a boy who couldn't have been more than fifteen years old. He had the same eyes as me, but his hair was much darker, and he looked to be on the chunky side. Just by looking at him, I could tell that we might have had different fathers. At least now, I knew what my brother looked like. I right-clicked on the photo and saved his picture in my picture folder.

Scrolling down, I began to read the story relating to his death. The article stated that he and a friend were in the treehouse built the year before by some of the boys of the home. The article mostly talked about the foster home's background and how it came to be through donations. It housed ten boys who were supervised by four adults. The deeper I got into the article, the more it talked about the accident. There were reports that Adam slipped from the edge, and another boy who was in the treehouse tried to pull him up, but was unable to. There was also a witness report that stated he heard two boys arguing, and when he looked over the fence to see what all the commotion was about, he saw Adam falling from the tree with another boy looking down on him as he fell.

There was no other information on the accident. When I got down to the bottom of the page, there was another picture. This time it was a group picture with the names underneath. From left to right, I began reading the names, Benjamin Wilson, Nathan Oliver, Adam Walker, Tommy Morgan, Peter Hewitt... My heart fell into my stomach as I looked at the picture, matching the name with the boy. It was Peter. Even though he was a lot thinner and younger then, there was no mistaking, it was him. He lived in the same foster home as my brother. He lied. He lied about my mother leaving. He lied about knowing my brother. Slamming the lid down on my computer, tears began filling my eyes. No wonder Peter didn't want to talk about his past. What really happened in that treehouse?

The night filtered into the morning, and my eyes were wide open. Every time I tried to close them, I saw Peter, and then I saw my brother's sad face. All I could think about was how scared he must have been when he fell from that treehouse. Who in their right mind would allow the boys to build it so high off the ground in the first place? It had to have been at least two stories high.

Knowing it was no use trying to fall asleep, I pushed from the bed and headed to the kitchen. Turning on the coffee maker, I sat on the barstool and watched as the amber liquid filled the pot. I wasn't sure if it was the lack of sleep or the fact that I was falling for a liar that had me numb. I couldn't stand the way I was feeling any longer. Heading to my room, I changed into my workout clothes, turned off the coffee maker, and headed out of the door, only to be stopped by Cop.

"Is there some place you need me to take you?" he asked, like it was no big deal.

"No," I said rudely. "I think you have done about enough."

"I can't let you leave by yourself, Lilly," he declared.

"I don't care. I'm going to the gym." I didn't wait for his response. I was totally over him and Peter, and especially the alpha-male bullshit.

The air was a little bit chillier than expected, making me wish I'd grabbed my light jacket. Needing to warm up, I began jogging at an even pace. On cue, Cop was right behind me. I thought it was funny watching him jog in heavy boots and jeans. Pushing myself a little harder, I turned my jog into a run as I rounded the corner. Turning my head, Cop was no longer behind me. This was my chance. Instead of ducking inside the gym, I decided to keep going. As I rounded the next corner, I waited for a moment to catch my breath and see if Cop would appear. Yep, he was gone. I was no longer cold. I slowed back down to a jogging pace and crossed the street. This was the first time in a long time that I actually had time to myself. With Cop camped outside my door and Peter breathing down my neck, I felt like my life was no longer my own.

I was only a few blocks away from Central Park. I thought it would be a good place to clear my head. I began jogging towards my favorite spot in the park. It was near Turtle Pond. Turning the corner to head that way, I should have been watching where I was going. Before I knew it, I was on the ground looking up at a muscular form wearing only shorts. The sun was blocking my view so that I couldn't see much of anything else. It was only after a hand stretched out and helped me to my feet that I realized who helped me.

"Pierre," I said, shocked.

"Lilly. It seems we keep running into each other," he said, smirking.

"Yeah, well, I won't let it happen again," I said, pulling myself from his embrace.

"It doesn't have to be that way, Lilly," he admitted.

"I know what you did to me. I know about the other girls too."

"I would never do anything to hurt you, Lilly. As I remember, you were more than willing to take what I was giving you," he clarified.

"I wasn't myself, I.... Oh, my God. Did you drug me?" I asked, knowing it was more than the wine that made me do what I did.

"Of course not, Lilly. I don't have to drug a woman to get her to fall into bed with me," he said, looking insulted by my accusation.

"Stay away from me, Pierre," I hissed, turning the other way to get away from him.

"I know what you think, Lilly. I would never hurt you." I heard him yelling behind me.

## CHAPTER TWENTY-FOUR
### *Lilly*

I hadn't heard from Peter in three days. There were so many times that I wanted to pick up the phone and call him, but my anger kept me from doing just that. I was sure that he knew I found out about him lying to me about my mom. Even though he was right about her not wanting to help herself, it still didn't make it right that he lied to me about her taking off. What hurt, even more was the fact that he lied about knowing my brother as well. Something happened that day in the treehouse. I wanted to know what he was hiding. Tossing my feeling aside, I dialed his number and waited for him to answer. Only he never did. The call went straight to voice mail.

After several failed attempts, I finally had enough courage to leave him a message. "We need to talk. Call me as soon as you get this."

~****~

Okay, now I was beginning to worry. It had been a week since I heard from Peter. Pacing back and forth, I started to think that something may have happened to him. My anger was beginning to turn into concern. Thoughts of something really bad happening to him began entering my mind. I knew he was doing some security work for someone in Washington. He said that he wasn't sure how long he would be gone. It was driving me crazy, not knowing what was going on with him.

Opening the front door to my condo, I tapped Cop on the shoulder. Even though I haven't said two words to him since the incident at the motel, this was something I needed to know. "Have you heard from Peter?" I asked as calmly as I could.

"No, I haven't. Peter said to get in touch with him only if there were any problems," Cop said.

"Well, there is a problem. I've called him at least a dozen times, and he hasn't returned any of my calls," I stated angrily.

"I'm sure he's fine, Lilly. He said he might be out of reach for a while. I'm sure he'll call when he can."

"Call him, Cop," I demand.

"I can't, Lilly," he refused.

I have never been more frustrated with anyone as I was with this man. Even as important as his work may have been, it was no excuse for not returning my calls. Maybe this was his way of saying he was done with me. I had two choices. I could wallow in my misery and hope that everything would be okay, and he would explain everything to me, or I could stop kidding myself and forget about him and move on. Pulling my phone from my pocket, I sent Peter the last text I would ever send to him. 'We're done.'

~****~

It had been two weeks since I heard from Peter. I erased his number from my contacts and threw out the t-shirt that I wore to keep him close. I even canceled the membership to Maximum Capacity. The only thing I couldn't get rid of was the nights I spent thinking of him as I cried myself to sleep. Each day was getting easier. I only caught myself thinking about him occasionally instead of every minute. The new shipment of artwork my parents sent from Paris was keeping me busy as well. Every day was the same. I'd get up, get ready for work, work all day, get home late, and go to bed. Once in a while, I would change it up and take a run around Central Park. I really needed to find a different gym. Even though running in the park kept me in shape, it did nothing for my social life.

Going over the invoices from the new shipment, I hear the bell chime from the front door. Brie had left to run some errands, so I knew I was the only one in the gallery. Pushing from my seat, I headed to the front to see who was there. Even though the gentleman's back was facing me, I knew exactly who it was.

"Pierre, I thought I made it perfectly clear that I didn't want you near me," I said, trying my best to stay calm.

"I remember what you said," he said as he began approaching my safe area. "I don't know what you've heard about me, but I think it's only fair that I am given a chance to defend myself."

"Say what you need to say, Pierre, and then you should leave," I advised nervously.

"I told you about the girl that I fell in love with during college and the rape charges her parents tried to place on me," he started as I watched him walk closer to me. "I didn't tell you about the other girls because they took back their claims against me shortly after. I have never forced myself on a woman, Lilly, and I certainly wouldn't drug you. You need to believe me."

He was in my space, only inches from my body. Cupping his hands on my cheeks, I could feel my body begin to submit to his touch. The way he was looking at me made me believe he was telling the truth. As he lowered his lips to mine, I should have stopped the kiss, but I couldn't. All I wanted was to feel something else besides the emptiness that had consumed me over the past two weeks. Wrapping my arms around his shoulders, I pulled him closer, needing to feel more of him. His hands slipped down my waist to the globes of my ass, where he rested them as he lifted me from the floor. I could feel the heat of his erection pulsating against my sex.

I was so totally consumed by his kiss that I hadn't realized we were heading to my office until my ass felt the cold, smooth surface of my desk. I knew whatever was going to happen needed to stop. Trying to break free, I moaned, "I can't do this, Pierre."

His hand gripped my hair as he pulled my head back, exposing the curve of my neck. "I need to have you, Lilly. You're all I think about," he said breathlessly.

Before I could maneuver away from him, he set me on the floor, spinning my body so that my chest was pressed against my desk. Holding me down with his hand against my back, he forced my arm back and held it firmly against the small of my back. With his other hand, he pulled my free arm I had tucked underneath me, and joined it with the other. As I fought to get away, his hand gripped my wrists tighter.

"Pierre, please let me go," I pleaded, trying to wiggle free.

"Not just yet, *amour*," he whispered softly in my ear.

I could feel his free hand on my thigh, pushing the hem of my skirt up, exposing my naked ass. The warmth of his hand began to slide between my legs, where I could feel his fingers moving the material of my panties to the side. As much as I didn't want this, I knew that I was wet. There was a slight tug, and I knew that he had just torn my panties from my body, leaving me bare for him. I shut my eyes and pleaded with him. "Please, no, Pierre."

I began to move frantically, but it was no use. He was so much stronger than I was. Hearing the sound of his zipper, I once again cried, "No, please stop."

"I know what you want, Lilly," he panted, pushing harder on my wrists to control my movements. "Soon..."

Feeling my stomach begin to churn, I felt the pressure against my hands begin to ease. I tried to push my body away from the desk, but instead, I found I could no longer move. My shoulders were burning with pain, and my wrists felt as though they were broken in half. I could feel my heart beating faster than it ever had. I tried again to push my body from the desk. Stumbling to the door, I heard the sound of grunts and moans. The only person I saw was Peter. He was lying on the floor, holding his hand across his side. Running to him, I knelt beside him to see that his face was beginning to show signs of bruising, and there was a small cut above his right eye.

"Peter," I sobbed. "Are you okay?"

"Yeah. Help me up," he said, trying to stand.

I helped him get to his feet while taking a better look at him. His hand was still clutching his side. Looking down, I could see that he had more than the bruising on his face. He was holding his side because he was trying to stop the blood that was seeping through his t-shirt. Moving his hand, I slowly lifted his blood-soaked shirt. The material clung to his body, causing him to wince in pain. "I have to see, Peter," I said softly.

Peter looked up at me and placed his blood-covered hand on my cheek. He didn't have to say anything for me to know that he was sorry. Placing my hand over his, I gave him a comforting look. Resuming the task at hand, I continued to lift his shirt to see the damage to his side. The blood was so thick. I knew for sure that the cut was deep. Tearing the sleeve from my blouse, I held it to the wound. The cut on his side was about six inches long. It wasn't as bad as I thought, but he would still most likely need stitches.

"Hold this here. I'm going to call 9-1-1," I said, looking at his pain-stricken face.

"No, Lilly, I'll be fine. Grab my phone for me. It's in my back pocket," he asked.

Reaching around to his backside, I pulled his cell from his pocket and put it in his free hand. With a swipe and a few touches to the screen, he held it to his ear and waited for someone to answer. "Sly, it's Peter. I've been hurt. Get the team together and meet me at the shop."

~****~

I don't know how I managed to do it, but I got Peter to the car. Brie still hadn't come back to the gallery by the time we left. I needed to call her to let her know what happened. Peter advised me what to share with her. I couldn't understand what the secret was about. Even though I didn't see what happened, I was pretty sure Pierre did this to him. He was the only other person at the gallery.

This whole thing could have been avoided if I hadn't told Josh that he didn't need to watch the gallery anymore.

He was reluctant to leave, but my yelling at him and threatening to call the police must have convinced him. Had he still been parked across the street, he would have noticed Pierre entering the gallery.

Cop was no longer perched in front of my door either. I told him the same thing yesterday that I told Josh. Peter must have known what I did because as soon as we got to the door, he said, "You shouldn't have forced my guys to leave."

"Yeah, well, you should have called me," I responded, taking my keys from my purse. This whole thing could have been avoided if he had just contacted me instead of making me worry about where he was and if anything bad happened to him.

Entering the condo, I helped Peter get settled on the couch. Turning from him once I knew he was as comfortable as he could be, I headed to the bathroom to see what I could find to patch him up. Returning with some gauze and tape and a bowl filled with antibacterial soap and water, I sat beside him to assess the damage to his side. As I began cleaning the blood from his wound, I couldn't understand why he was being so stubborn about going to the hospital.

The hospital was way more equipped to take care of him than I was.

Looking over to him with concern, I said, "Peter, you really need to go to the hospital. This wound needs stitches."

"Let me worry about that. Do you have nylon thread and a needle?" he asked.

"I don't have nylon thread, Peter. I might have a needle, though," I said.

"How about dental floss?" he asked.

Nodding, I got up and walked back to the bedroom to gather what he wanted. There was a bottle of vodka sitting on the coffee table when I returned. I could see that he drank about a quarter of the contents. If he planned on stitching himself up, he needed to stop drinking; otherwise, he wouldn't be able to concentrate on what he was doing.

After he took another swig from the bottle, I pulled it from his hand. "Peter, if you continue to drink like that, you aren't going to be much good stitching yourself up."

"I'm not going to do it, Lilly, you are," he advised me, pulling the vodka bottle from my grasp.

"I can't stitch you up, Peter," I said nervously. There was no way he was going to make me do this.

"Then I guess I'll just bleed to death."

I wasn't sure if he was just playing me or if he actually might bleed to death. With the amount of blood on his shirt and the fact that he was still bleeding, I knew he could bleed to death. I didn't know the first thing about sewing up a wound. The only thing I did know was that whatever was being used needed to be sterile. Taking the needle between my fingers, I walked to the kitchen to find the lighter that I used to light my candles. Pulling it from the drawer, I ignited it and placed the flame over the tip of the needle for a couple of seconds until I felt satisfied that any germs living there were dead.

Sitting beside Peter, I pulled out a long piece of floss from its container and threaded it through the eye of the needle. With the threaded needle in one hand, I took the bottle of vodka from Peter with the other and took a big swallow. I needed all the courage I could get. Peter clenched his teeth with a moan as the first stab broke his skin. I began stitching him up while he gave me instructions on how to loop the string to make a knot. By the time I had finished with my handiwork, I had looped and knotted a total of fifteen stitches. Covering the wound with a large gauze pad, I taped it to his skin and wrapped an ace bandage around his waist to keep it in place. Even though I wasn't a doctor, I had to admit I did a pretty good job.

Peter was resting on the couch when his phone began to vibrate. Pushing from the chair I was occupying beside him, I picked up his phone, noticing that Sly was the caller. Swiping my hand across the screen, I said, "Hello."

"This doesn't sound like Peter," he said sarcastically.

"He's resting," I said.

"Well, when Sleeping Beauty wakes from his nap, let him know that I've contacted all the guys. They'll all be at the shop in an hour."

Leaning over to place the cell back on the table, I saw two very angry eyes staring back at me. "That was Sly. He said the guys would be at the shop in an hour," I said, watching him push his body in a sitting position.

"Thanks," he said, looking around for his soiled t-shirt.

"If you're looking for your shirt, I threw it away. It was disgusting," I said, turning up my nose. "I might have one for you in the bedroom."

Searching my room, I found one of his t-shirts at the bottom of my drawer. Thinking that I should have thrown this one away along with the other, I held it to my nose to breathe in his scent. As much as I wanted to forget about him, this was the one thing I couldn't get rid of. It was the last piece of him I had. Making him think about what he lost, I sprayed a small amount of my favorite perfume on the front. I wanted him to be reminded of me.

Peter was standing near the window looking out over the city when I entered the room. Careful not to scare him, I walked beside him and held out his shirt. Taking the shirt from me, I could feel the pull he had on my body. Even though I knew we could never be together, I still wanted him. Letting go of the last piece of him, I watched as he slowly pulled his t-shirt on. Even though he was in pain, I could see a small smile on his face as he took in the scent I left behind.

Turning towards me, he rubbed his thumb across my lips. My eyes closed, feeling the pain in my heart, knowing that we could never be together. Opening my eyes, I could see that he was no longer there. With my head dipped, I asked the one question that would break us. "Did you do it, Peter? Did you kill my brother?"

Feeling pressure in my chest, I looked over to the front door, where he stopped. He didn't turn so I could see his face. I had my answer when he walked out the door without a word.

# CHAPTER TWENTY-FIVE
## *Peter*

Leaving Lilly was the hardest thing I ever did. Somehow, I knew she would eventually find out about my past and what happened to her brother. I knew that Diana wouldn't be able to keep her mouth shut. It didn't matter how hard I tried to keep the truth from her, it came out anyway.

On the way to the shop, I called the one person I trusted with my past, the one person who could take care of what should have been taken care of a long time ago.

"DFS, this is Matt," he answered.

"I need your help, Matt," I said, gripping the wheel tighter.

"I take it she found out," he said.

"Yeah, that's why I need you to take care of Diana Walker," I said with gritted teeth, being beyond pissed.

"What do you need from me, Peter?" he questioned.

"I need her to go away for a long time. I don't care how you do it, just get it done. I'm done messing with this bitch."

Pulling up to the shop, I could see that all the guys were there. Putting my car into park, I felt a prick of pain as I got out. This meeting was going to keep Lilly safe once and for all. That asshole was never going to lay his hands on her again. When I received her text, I didn't know what to make of it. All I knew was that I needed to get my ass on the first flight back to New York. When I found out from Cop that Lilly threatened to call the police if they didn't leave her alone, it only made matters worse. I knew the only reason she would act like that was because she knew. She found out about my past and her brother. As much as I wanted to get in touch with her, if only to just hear her voice, I couldn't risk putting her in danger. The people I was dealing with in Washington would make sure everything I loved was taken away from me if things didn't go as planned. I couldn't risk them finding out about Lilly. She was the only good thing in my life.

When I opened the door to the shop, the guys were hanging back relaxing. As soon as they saw me, that all changed. They knew something was up, and it wasn't good. I could always count on my guys to know when something bad was about to hit the fan. Heading to the soundproof conference room, I knew my men were right behind me. The only time we ever used the room was when I felt the need to keep conversations private. Anyone who ever tried to home in on our discussions would get nothing other than an earful of static.

Waiting until they took their places, I gathered my thoughts. After I heard someone from my group clear their throat, I began my explanation for the meeting.

"Pierre got to Lilly," I began, looking in the direction of Cop and Josh. I knew it wasn't their fault. Eventually, they would have been sighted, and the end result would have been the same. Lilly would have been left without protection. "He showed up at the gallery. Somehow, he must have known that there was no one around protecting her, and he found his window of opportunity. If I hadn't walked in the gallery and heard her scream, who knows how far he would have taken it with her." Scanning the room, I could see my guys lower their heads in shame. "Look, I'm not blaming anyone for what happened. We need to work as a team and fix this."

"What do you want us to do, boss?" Hawk asked, lifting his head.

"Find him," I demanded. "I don't care what it takes, I want him."

"You okay, bro?" Hawk asked, noticing my gritted teeth as I stood up.

"Yeah, just a little inconvenience from that motherfucker," I snapped.

All of the guys filed out of the room except for Hawk. Out of all the men I served with and worked with, he was the closest thing I had to a brother. Closing the door, he turned to me with that look I knew so well. Taking a seat on the other end of the conference table, he said his piece. "Peter, you and I have known each other for a long time. I know that something is going on with you, and it goes deeper than this guy stalking Lilly. It's not like you to let someone get a piece of you. Are you going to spill, or do I need to knock the shit out of you?"

Hawk always had a way of getting his point across. There were no secrets between us. "Lilly knows about my past. I don't know how much her fucked-up mom told her, but she knows I had something to do with her brother's death."

"You have to stop beating yourself up over what happened over fifteen years ago. That kid wasn't right. You said so yourself. Who calls someone a 'Coward' and then just releases their grip? He wanted to die, Peter. There's no way you could have known he was going to let go," he said.

"You're right. I have been off my game. I need to take care of this shit before it rips me apart." Standing, I patted Hawk on the shoulder before leaving the conference room. This thing between Lilly and me had to stop now. Sooner or later, she needed to know the truth. It didn't matter anymore, because either way, she was going to hate me, but at least this way she would know the truth.

As I was leaving the shop, my phone began to vibrate in my pocket. Reaching behind me, I pulled it out to see

Matt's contact on my screen. "Hey, Matt," I said, grunting as I painfully got into my car.

"That little problem you wanted me to take care of for you has already been taken care of. It seems Diana Walker knows how to find trouble on her own. She was arrested this morning for possession, and aiding and abetting a felon wanted on drug charges. It looks like you won't be hearing from her for a while," Matt said.

"Let me guess. The felon was Bud Colver?" I asked.

"Yeah, how did you know?" Matt questioned.

"Lucky guess. Couldn't have happened to a nicer guy," I said, feeling like things were finally going my way.

~****~

It was nice to know that at least one of my problems was taken care of. The nice thing about it was that I didn't have to get my hands dirty to get it done. Driving to Lilly's place, all I could think about was how I would tell her the truth about her brother. I needed to listen to Hawk's advice and remember that it wasn't my fault. As much as I hated the kid at the time, I wasn't the one who let go. Looking back on that day, maybe he did have a death wish. I just hoped that I could convince Lilly of that. Just like that, I remembered something I saved when I was a kid. I kept it as a constant reminder that I was never going to be that kid again. Turning around and heading back the other way, I accelerated onto the 9A, taking a left onto I-78 to the Holland Tunnel.

Once I reached my building on Morgan Street, I slipped into my parking spot and rushed up to my apartment. There was no turning back now. Heading to my closet, I pulled out the shoebox that held all of my childhood memories. Most of them were too painful to forget. Tossing the lid on the bed, I lifted the items, remembering everything about each as I pulled them out one by one. I didn't know why I felt the need to keep these reminders of how shitty my childhood was. Maybe it was a reminder that I never wanted to be that boy again. I never wanted to be that helpless.

Putting everything back inside, I tucked the box under my arm and headed out the door. Grabbing my helmet, I opted to take my bike instead of the Camaro. There was something about riding my bike that always helped me clear my head. It was like a rush, being free. Opening one of the compartments, I tucked the box inside and got on. Revving up the engine, I could already feel the pressure inside my gut start to ease.

Reaching Lilly's building thirty minutes later, I parked my bike next to her Lexus. I would have parked my bike out on the street, but I was hoping that after I told her what needed to be said, she would understand and let me show her just how much I needed her. Hopefully, it wasn't wishful thinking on my part. I didn't know what I would do if I ever lost Lilly.

Knocking lightly on the door, I waited for her to answer. I must have woken her up. Her hair was tied back in a messy pony, and she didn't have any make-up on. God, she looked sexy as hell. She was only wearing a t-shirt and a pair of boy shorts. I was about ready to scold her for answering the door with barely any clothing on, but I knew I needed to remain calm. Watching her step aside, I walked past her and took a seat on the couch while placing the tattered box on the table.

Sitting across from me and tucking her legs under her, she asked softly, "What are you doing here, Peter?"

Patting my hand on the couch, wanting her next to me, I said, "I'm ready to tell you everything, Lilly. I can't stand the way things are between us. I'm tired of keeping secrets from you."

"Okay," she said, taking her place next to me.

I didn't know where to begin. She must have sensed my uneasiness, because she placed her hand on my shoulder, taking my hand into hers with the other. "I know this is hard for you Peter. I just want to know the truth… about everything."

Taking in a deep breath, I began. "My mom was a drug addict. Just like yours. Only I wasn't so lucky. She died when I was five. We lived in a rundown apartment in Brooklyn. It wasn't much, but it was the only home I knew. She got some bad stuff. She never woke up. For days, maybe weeks, I stayed with her, hoping she would. The police found me huddled next to her cold body. I always tried to keep her warm, but she was always cold. Needless to say, they took me away from her and placed me in a foster home."

"Is that where you met my brother?" she asked softly.

"Not right away. I was eight when he showed up. None of the other kids liked him. They thought he was messed up. I felt sorry for him, so I became his friend. His only friend. As we got older, he changed. It was like he hated everyone, even me. Everyone was afraid of him. He made threats against the other boys if they didn't give him their lunch or do what he asked. He was a bully. He grew to be really big. That's when our friendship ended. I was just a scrawny little kid. Even as I got older, I remained thin while he kept getting bigger and bigger. I hated that place. I swore when I was old enough, I would go into the military and become something. I always watched those commercials on TV with the 'Be all that you can be' shit." I could tell by the look on Lilly's face that she was beginning to understand how bad my childhood really was.

Swiping a tear from her face, she said, "I'm sorry, Peter. I'm glad you're telling me this."

I wasn't sure how glad she would be after I told her the rest of the truth. Placing my hand on her cheek, I began again. "Somehow, the rest of the boys, including me, convinced the foster parents to let us build a treehouse. One of them sided with us, thinking it would bring all of us closer if we did something together. Looking back, I wish we never built that fucking thing." Gritting my teeth, I lowered my head as I forked my hands through my hair. "When I turned seventeen, I got a camera, one of those fancy digital ones. It was the best day of my life. I never had anything so nice. At first, I took pictures of everything. Then I only took pictures of what Adam was doing with the other boys. I thought if I had pictures of what he was doing to us, he would get in trouble, and they would send him away."

Standing, I walked over to the window to look out at the Manhattan sky. I could feel Lilly coming up behind me, placing her arms around my waist. "Peter, are you okay?" she asked.

"Yeah. I just needed a little breather," I said, turning towards her.

"What happened next, Peter?" she asked.

Taking her by the hand, I walked her back to the couch, pulling her onto my lap. If I was going to get the rest out, I wanted to make sure she was close to me. "My camera went missing. Adam took over everything, even the treehouse. None of us could go up to it unless he gave his permission. I knew that he found out what I was doing. I knew my camera was in the treehouse. He and some of the other boys went down the street to get ice cream. I thought that was my chance to get my camera back. I went up to the treehouse and searched for it. I found it hidden between two boards, but I wasn't quick enough. Adam was already up the stairs. He saw me and started laying into me. He started telling me what a fuck-up I was and what a whore my mom was. He said she gave me up because I was in the way when she fucked one of her Johns. I got so mad at him. All I could see was fire. The camera fell out of my hand and landed close to the edge of the treehouse. I needed to get it, so I pushed him off of me, only I pushed him too hard. He went over the edge. He was hanging on with one hand. I reached for him to grab my hand. He did. I just stared at him. I couldn't pull him up. There was something in his eyes. I should have known." My body began to tremble as I remembered the look on his face before he let go.

"Oh my God, Peter. It wasn't your fault. You didn't know that by pushing him, he was going to fall. You were angry at him," she said, tears filling her eyes.

"There's something else you need to know, Lilly," I said as I reached for the box and pulled out the memory card that used to be in my camera all those years ago.

Handing her laptop to her, I waited as she booted it up. I gave her the card containing my childhood memories. As she pushed the card into the side of her computer, the pictures began loading one by one. I watched as she clicked through each one. There was so much love in the first few pictures, but as she continued to click forward, the darkness began to appear. It was only when she got to the last few pictures that she had seen the truth. That day in the treehouse, during the fight, my camera must have landed on the shutter button when it fell out of my hand and hit the floor. It was still set on auto mode, so it took picture after picture of what happened. The only thing that it was unable to record was Adam's last word before he let go of my hand.

Lilly's eyes were fixed on the last pictures when Adam fell to his death. His eyes weren't the only thing that said it all. It was also in the smile that the camera captured as he fell. Placing my hand on her shoulder, I wanted to comfort her. Her body was quivering as the tears spilled from her. I knew the truth would be hard on her. Turning her body to mine, I took her in my arms and held her close.

"For so long, I blamed myself for his death. I should have never pushed him. I should have known better, I was older," I confessed.

"There's no way you could have known that he was going to let go. I could see it in his eyes, Peter, he wanted to end his life," she said between sobs.

I wasn't sure how much time had passed while sitting with Lilly cuddled like a child in my arms. Even though the weight of the world had been lifted off my shoulders, a heavy load had been added to hers. The family she thought she could save ended up being her worst defeat. The last thing I wanted was to hurt her.

# CHAPTER TWENTY-SIX
## *Lilly*

Sometime after midnight, Peter carried me to bed. I knew that the stuff he was going to tell me about my brother would be hard to handle. I was prepared to break things off with him, thinking that he killed my brother. What I didn't know was that he really didn't. Even though he blamed himself for pushing Adam, Adam ultimately caused his own death by letting go.

Rolling over to my side, I looked over to Peter, who seemed more at peace with himself than he had ever been. I could only imagine what he went through as a kid, dealing with his mother's death and being placed with strangers. It also made me realize how lucky I was that my life turned out the way that it did. Pushing up to my feet, I felt the need to reach out to my parents. Quietly exiting the bedroom so I wouldn't wake Peter, I went to the kitchen to call my mom.

After two rings, I heard my mom's happy voice. "Hey, sweetheart, is everything okay?"

"Yeah, I just miss you guys," I said, twisting a loose piece of hair between my fingers.

"We miss you too, Lilly. Your father and I are talking about coming to New York next week. We haven't seen you since the opening of Séduire. We thought it was time," she said excitedly.

"Really? That would be wonderful," I responded, raising my arm and pulling it back in a 'yes' motion.

Ending the call with my mom, I heard Peter walk up behind me. The warmth of his body enveloped mine as he placed a small tender kiss along my neckline to my shoulder, sending goosebumps down my body. Turning to face him, I saw a smirk on his face that I had grown to love. Placing my hands on his shoulders, I rose to my toes and kissed him on the lips. God, how I loved his lips. Without warning, Peter had me up off my feet, hauling me back to the bedroom. Somehow, something about this moment seemed so right. After everything that we had been through, he was the only person I wanted to be with. Even when we were apart, all I wanted was him.

Peter gently placed me on the bed while carefully kneeling between my legs with his massive torso leaning over me. With his hands on either side of my head, he bent lower and kissed me on the lips. His tongue gently swept across my mouth, causing my lips to part. I was engulfed by his warmth. Reaching down his rippled abs, I slid my hand down the perfect 'V' and under his red boxers. Moving them over his hips and over his tight ass, I gripped his cheeks, pulling him even closer to me. My legs spread wider as I allowed him better access to my sex. I could feel the grinding movement of his hips as his hand glided down my chest, between my breasts, to the area just above my belly button. In one swift motion, Peter pulled my t-shirt up over my head and placed his hungry mouth over my taut nipple. Surges of pleasure radiated from the tip of my nipple to my core as Peter continued to lap and suck the hard peak. A soft moan escaped my lips, releasing the desire I had for this man.

Moving his hand lower down my body, he placed his palm on my mound while inserting his finger inside my channel. My back began to arch, and my hips began to rock, needing to feel more of him as he pushed deeper inside. I sighed in frustration needing more. "Peter, please, I need you inside me."

My body was just about to give way when Peter flipped me over, pulling up on my hips. In one precise movement, Peter entered me, filling me with his hard cock. My walls began to stretch as I tried to accommodate his large rod. As he adjusted my hips so that he could get better penetration, I felt the onset of my release as the tip of his dick glided over my g-spot. "God, you feel so good, Lilly," I heard him say as I continued to hold tight to my impending explosion. "I'm going to fuck you until you scream my name," he said, pushing deeper inside me.

When I was on the verge of letting go, once again, Peter pulled from inside me. "On your back, Lilly," he demanded.

When I rolled over to my back, he opened my legs so that he could resume his place inside me. My heart was pounding, and my breath was becoming short. Just a few more thrusts, and I'd be his. Keeping me wanting, Peter slowed his rhythm and pulled completely out before thrusting back inside me. My body was hot and sweaty, in need of release. Opening my eyes, I saw Peter's eyes upon me. His hands lifted mine above my head, holding them in place. Adjusting his hold, he moved my hands together and gripped them with one of his own. Brushing his free hand across my cheek, Peter lowered his head and kissed me passionately on the lips. I could feel the beating of his heart. He broke the kiss, looking at me with compassion as he swiped his thumb slowly across my bottom lip. There was something in his eyes that I had never seen before, something pure and comforting. His eyes closed for only a moment when he uttered affectionately, "I love you, Lilly." It was only after I saw the only tear he had ever shed fall from his eye that I felt the same way.

~****~

After three bouts of lovemaking, Peter finally left my condo. As much as he didn't want to, he had things to take care of. He said there would be no more secrets between us, so when I asked what he needed to take care of, he told me that he and his team was going after Pierre. Even though I was glad that he told me, I was also afraid that something could go wrong. Pierre was no dummy. And seeing firsthand what he was capable of made me worry even more. To ease my anxiety, Peter said that he would check in with me to let me know that he was okay.

Needing to get things done myself, I decided to head out to the gallery to take care of a few things. When I grabbed my keys, Cop was back outside my door. I felt bad over the way I treated him the other day. I would never have called the police on him, or any of Peter's men.

Turning to him, I said, "Cop, about what I said before, about calling the police, I didn't mean it. I was just so angry with Peter."

"I know, Lilly. We've all had our share of anger sometime or another," he replied, referring to Peter.

"I'm heading to the gallery, just so you know," I said, smiling at him.

"I'll follow you down," Cop said as we entered the elevator.

Just as we hit the main floor, I forgot that I left a file on a new artist in my car. "I'll meet you out front; I just need to grab something from my car."

"I can come with you," Cop volunteered.

"Don't be silly. It will only take a sec," I reassured him.

"Okay," he nodded reluctantly.

"See you out front," I confirmed before the elevator door closed.

Pushing the lower level, I waited for the elevator to stop at the level where my car was. Even though I loved where I lived, I wished my parking spot was a little closer to the elevator. Walking to where my car was parked, I began to get this eerie feeling that I wasn't the only one in the parking garage. Increasing my pace, my walk turned into a slow jog as I headed in the direction of my car. As I placed my hand on the handle of my car door, thinking that I was safe, I heard his voice behind me. "Hello, Lilly. We never got to finish what we started at the gallery."

My skin began to crawl with the sound of his voice so close to my ear. When I tried to pull the door open, his hand pressed against the window, causing the door to slam shut. Taking a swing at him, I tried to throw him off balance so I could at least get away long enough to climb one floor up to where Cop would be waiting for me. My judgment must have been off because he got one in first, causing my light to turn to dark.

~****~

My head was throbbing as my eyes slowly opened. I wasn't sure where I was, but from what I could see, it was a bedroom with very expensive furnishings. I tried to sit up, but my hands were bound to the headboard with handcuffs. Looking at the end of the bed, I could see that the clothes I was wearing were no longer on me. The only thing covering my body was a sheer nightgown. My head was a little foggy, but I remembered hearing Pierre's voice behind me and then the feeling of his fist across my cheek. I wished I had listened to Cop and let him follow me to my car. What the hell was I thinking?

Laying my head back on the pillow, I knew an escape attempt was useless. The cuffs were too tight around my wrists. I couldn't wiggle out of them if I tried. The only thing I could do was wait until someone showed up.

Hearing what sounded like the unlocking of the door, I raised my head from the pillow to see if I could tell who was coming. When the door opened, it was Pierre standing in the doorway. Holding a tray, he walked towards the bed. "You're awake. Good. I brought you something to eat. I knew you would be hungry since you have been out for a while."

"What do you want from me, Pierre?" I asked, pulling on my restraints.

"For us to be together. I knew from the first moment I saw you in Paris that I should have never let you go," he said regretfully as he placed the tray on the nightstand. "Now, if you behave, I'll uncuff you so you can sit up."

Nodding my head, I watched as he pulled a small key from his pocket. Unlatching the cuff, he helped me sit up by putting his hands under my arms and lifting me high up in the bed. Removing the dome from the plate, he began to prepare my meal. Scooping up a small portion onto a fork, he looked to me and said, "Open, Lilly."

I had no other choice but to open my mouth as he gently placed the food between my lips. Unsure of what he was feeding me, I took in the flavor. It was surprisingly good.

With each bite, my stomach began to fill. I was about halfway through my meal when I told him, "No more."

"Very well," he said. "Even though you didn't eat very much, I will let it go this time." He turned and placed the dome back over the remaining food on the plate. "I'm going to get this out of here, then I will be back to draw you a bath."

I tried to hit him with my free hand, but that only made him angry. Pulling me down on the bed, his body was now over mine. I tried to wiggle free, but he took hold of my arm and re-secure my hand in the handcuff. Looking down on me, he lowered his mouth to mine. I shook my head back and forth, not wanting any part of him touching me. He clasped his hand on my chin, holding my head in place, causing me to stop my movement. Lowering his head inches from mine, he whispered calmly, "It would behoove you to stop fighting me, Lilly. I'm not letting you go this time."

His lips lowered to mine, and he kissed me with such force that I could taste a hint of blood as my teeth dug into my lip. With a triumphant smirk, he pushed from me and gathered the tray, leaving the room. I wanted so badly to wipe the grime from my lips, but I couldn't. Instead, I used the skin of my upper arm and transferred it from my lips to another part of my body.

My only hope now was that I could find a way to get away from him when he came back for my bath.

# CHAPTER TWENTY-SEVEN
## *Peter*

Totally beside myself, I couldn't believe this was happening again. I was no closer to getting Pierre than I was a few days ago. The only difference was that now he had Lilly. I had to find her. Hawk had this funny feeling that Pierre might not have moved from the apartment he had rented across the street from Lilly's place. There was one thing I could always count on, and that was Hawk's instincts. It was like he knew the actions of a stalker; more importantly, Pierre Marchand's.

It was no surprise when we broke into Pierre's apartment that we had all the evidence we needed to prove that this guy was a nut job and needed to be locked up. I had never seen so many photos of Lilly as he had hanging on his walls. What really made me angry was some of the photos were of her naked body. I couldn't understand how he could have gotten so close to her to take all of those pictures, not until I found his telescope pointed directly at Lilly's bedroom window. Even though I knew that Lilly would never stand in front of the window to get dressed, I knew exactly how he was able to capture her. The mirror on her dresser was positioned at just the right angle that he could see her reflection from the mirror. He then used a high-resolution telescopic lens to get the pictures he wanted. It made me sick just thinking about him jacking off while he watched her.

While I felt like I was ready to lose it, Hawk walked up to me with a folder. "You need to take a look at this, Peter."

Opening the folder, I saw a deed to some place in Southampton. The name on the deed didn't match Pierre's, so I had no clue why I was even looking at it. It was only when Hawk pointed out the trustee that I began to put two and two together. Pierre's mom must have remarried but kept her maiden name. She was the owner of the estate and the current executor of his trust. Scanning the rest of the documents in the folder, more information was revealed. It was beginning to make sense. Pierre Marchand was tied to Lilly in more ways than one. "We need to get to this house in Southampton," I said. "If he has her, that's the only place he would take her."

I took four of my men with me to Southampton: Hawk, Cop, Sly, and Ryan. I figured with the five of us, we could take Pierre down and get Lilly. I didn't know what to expect when we got there. I just wanted to be prepared for anything that could happen. Getting into our vehicles, Hawk rode with me in my Camaro while Sly and Ryan rode with Cop in his power truck. I was the lead vehicle, so I took the fastest route I knew of to get there as quickly as possible.

There was an accident on I-495, causing us to cut across to Hwy 27. It wasn't the best route, but it would be the fastest. I could feel Hawk's eyes on me as my speeds were well above the posted limit. "I know what you're thinking, Hawk. I can't waste any time. It's two fucking hours to Southampton, and I need to cut as much time as possible."

"You didn't hear me say anything," Hawks said, raising his hands in surrender.

"You didn't have to. I could see it on your face," I retorted.

Nothing more was said about my excess speed. It was already late when we left Manhattan, so by the time we reached Southampton, it was dark. The only thing we had to go by was the address. I wasn't familiar with the town, so I only had the GPS to direct us to the right location.

Once we arrived at our destination, the large house came into view. I wasn't sure what I was expecting, but seeing the size of the house, I knew it was going to be an obstacle. Lilly could be anywhere inside. Our only advantage was that it was dark, and hopefully, we would be able to move around the property unnoticed.

I pulled the car around the block, thinking this was our best bet. Another problem I saw was the gate in front of the house. This was another reason for us parking around the block. If I had to guess, the property was outfitted with surveillance cameras. I didn't see any when driving past the front gates, but that didn't mean there weren't any scattered along the perimeter of the house.

Grabbing everything we might need, we headed to the vine-covered fence just north of the entrance gate. As we scaled the brick and iron fence, I noticed most of the lights were burning on the lower floor while only one light on the second floor was on. Resting my body on the top edge of the fence, I pulled out my binoculars to scan the house. I couldn't see any movements through the windows on the lower floor.

Moving my focus to the upper floor, particularly the room where the lights were on, I tried to see if I could see any movements through the door leading to the balcony outside. Focusing the lens, I captured it. There she was, sitting in a chair near what looked to be a vanity. I could see movement behind her. Moving my sights, I just about lost it. Standing behind her, Pierre had his hands on her. Even though he was just brushing her hair, the thought of him being so close to her caused me to snap. I almost gave away our position when Pierre looked my way. Lowering my body in a prone position, I didn't move. Keeping my eyes on him at all times, I watched as he moved back to Lilly and resumed his task. Watching him touch her, caress her hair with each stroke of the brush, and then kiss her tenderly on the cheek made me lose it completely.

I couldn't watch anymore. This motherfucker just took his last breath. Aiming my rifle at his frame, I waited for him to move so I could get a clear shot. With my hand on the trigger, I watched as he slowly turned my way. This was my chance, only I didn't get it. Hawk placed his hand on the barrel of my gun and lowered it, causing me to miss my chance. Looking at him, I whispered with gritted teeth, "What the fuck?" Taking his cue, I looked over to where he was pointing. I was so focused on Lilly that I didn't notice the older man and woman leaving the house through the front door. They must have been servants by the way they were dressed.

I waited until the two of them got into their car and drove off before I tried for another shot. My chance never came. Lilly was no longer at the vanity, nor was Pierre. I knew we needed to get closer. Jumping down from the edge of the fence, I stayed low to the ground, watching the sedan pull through the gates. I wasn't sure what the house was equipped with, but I couldn't take the chance of activating motion sensors. My guys were close behind me. I signaled for Sly and Ryan to head to the front door, while Hawk, Cop, and I headed around back.

Once we were inside, Cop went to search for the basement while the rest of us waited. Once the power was cut, we knew Cop had found the fuse box. Even though we were unfamiliar with the house, we did our best work in the dark. Ascending the stairs two at a time, Hawk and I headed to where we thought the room where Lilly was being held was. Staying low to the ground, I reached up and turned the knob to the door. It was dark, but the light shining through the glass patio doors from the moon told me we were in the right place. Inching along the floor, I could hear sounds coming from another room, which I assumed was either a bathroom or a closet.

Something happened because all of a sudden, the lights came on in the room. I heard a noise coming from the closed door. Aiming my gun, I waited for it to open. As the door slowly opened, my heart began to pound. Pierre held Lilly by the waist while her hands were cuffed behind her.

"Peter," she cried.

"It's over, Pierre. Let her go." I hissed.

"Nice try. I would say you are at a little disadvantage," he sneered, holding Lilly steady as he displayed the gun he was holding on her.

"I know all about you, Pierre, I know about this house, the gallery in Paris, your parents," I said, needing to keep his mind focused on me.

"You don't know anything, asshole."

"I know that you lost everything. I know your parents lost the gallery in Paris and that Lilly's parents bought it. But most of all, I know about Candice. I know what her parents did to you. Lilly is not Candice, Pierre," I replied, knowing my words were beginning to get to him.

"Shut up! You know nothing about Candice and what we had. Lilly is exactly like Candice. She's sweet and compassionate. Most of all, she's mine," he choked.

I needed to do something fast. I could see the fear in Lilly's eyes. The way he was pushing the gun into her side, I knew I didn't have much time. Hearing Hawk's voice through my earpiece, I wait for his signal as the door opened, drawing Pierre off balance. This was my only chance. Instead of shooting him with the rifle at my side, I grabbed for my Glock and pointed slowly, pulling the trigger, sending several rounds his way. Everything began to move in slow motion as I watched Lilly fall to the floor. Pierre must have let her go. Looking straight at me, he lifted his gun and pointed it in my direction. It was only then that I heard another shot, which landed directly between his eyes. Looking over to my left, I saw Ryan standing just inside the patio door with his rifle still aimed at Pierre.

Pushing up to my feet, I ran to where Lilly's body lay motionless. Making sure she wasn't hit during the gunfire, I pulled her close to me. Feeling her breath on my face, I yelled over to Hawk and demanded uncontrollably, "Get these fucking handcuffs off her."

Hawk was at my side in seconds, working the cuffs off her hands. The minute her hands were free, they wrapped tightly around my neck. I heard the soft sound of her voice. "I knew you would come for me."

~****~

I spent the longest hour of my life in that Godforsaken place while the police questioned us. All I wanted to do was get Lilly home, far away from here. Hawk drove the Camaro while I sat in the back seat, holding Lilly close to me. It was the most excruciating ride I had ever taken. My legs were cramped beyond belief, and my shoulders ached from being jammed into the back seat of a car that my big body had no right to be in. But being with Lilly made everything better. I would withstand any discomfort as long as I knew she would be with me always.

I decided to take her to my place instead of her condo. I didn't know how she felt about it, but I didn't give her a choice given the circumstances. Hawk pulled into my designated parking spot two and a half hours later. Lilly was resting on my lap with her head tucked in the crook of my neck. Hawk pushed the seat up, and I handed her off to him while trying to get out of the sardine can, known as the back seat. Stretching my cramped legs and my sore shoulders, I looked at Hawk and asked, "Can you take her up for me? I need to work out these kinks."

"You bet," he replied as I handed him the keys to my apartment.

"Oh, and Hawk, no funny stuff. That's my girl," I said firmly.

Walking the length of the parking garage, I began thinking about everything that happened and how things could have turned out differently had I taken the shot I initially intended to take. I was so thankful that Hawk had my back. Just like now. Feeling the blood flowing again in my legs, I headed up to my apartment to check in on my girl. I needed comfort, even if it meant only holding her near.

Removing the rest of my gear, I headed to the bedroom where I knew Lilly would be. Looking down at her,

her eyes were still closed, she was the most gorgeous woman I had ever seen. Pulling off my own clothing, I slipped in beside her, pulling her warm body next to mine. This is the way it should be, her next to me. Always.

## CHAPTER TWENTY-EIGHT
### *Lilly*

I could feel something warm pressed against my body. I only hoped it wasn't the man I thought it was. I was afraid to open my eyes to find Pierre lying next to me instead of the man I had fallen in love with. Opening one eye first and then the other, I looked around the room to find that I was no longer in Pierre's house. I'd seen this room before. It belonged to Peter. Shooting to a sitting position, making sure I was fully awake, I looked over my shoulder to find Peter lying next to me, reaching across the empty area I just occupied. I had never seen anything so funny as watching Peter panic when he no longer felt my body next to his. Lying back, I took hold of his arm and snuggled it around my body as I laid my head on his chest. "Don't ever do that, Lilly. From now on, say something, anything, to let me know you haven't left. Matter of fact, I'll just tie you to the bed, so you never leave," he said jokingly.

"You did not just say that," I said, slapping him on the chest.

"Sorry, bad joke, but now that I'm awake..." he said, lifting the covers to have a look at his manhood. "I think..."

Before he could finish his sentence, my body was over his, straddling his taut stomach. I pushed my hips back slightly, feeling his early morning arousal. Leaning back, I reached around my back and placed my hand on his hard shaft. Trying hard to contain my laughter, I watched the cutest smile ever fill his face. I scooted my body further down his hard muscles until I was face to face with his impressive cock. As I tugged his underwear off his hips, he lifted his bottom to assist my efforts. Flinging his boxers to the floor, I began my descent down his beautiful mass. Taking my time, I slowly circled my tongue around the head while working my hand up and down the base.

I heard the sound of approval when deep moans of pleasure fill the room. Opening my mouth, I took him as far as I could before lapping my tongue around the head. I could feel the pulsation beneath my hand as I continued to stroke him slowly. His body began to move with my mouth, pushing his dick deeper and deeper inside. I opened my throat in order to take more of him. Increasing my movements, I worked his cock in and out of my mouth. I could feel his release getting closer as his grip on my hair began to tighten. I focused only on the pleasure I was giving him and not the discomfort he was causing me.

"Fuck," he cried out as his seed spilled inside my mouth.

Climbing up his body, I trailed soft kisses along the hard ridges of his abs to the broad expansion of his chest. It was only after I was splayed across his hard body that he flipped me over onto my back. My body was inflamed from the heat of desire that was burning inside. His lips crashed down on mine, feeding the fire that was ready to explode inside me. Our kiss deepened, causing the moisture of my sex to pool between my legs. His hand slowly glided down my torso, stopping at my cleft. I knew what he felt; I knew how my touch affected him. My legs parted, giving him the access that he needed as he dipped two fingers inside me. I could feel every nerve in my body come alive the deeper he sank inside. Unable to hold on any longer, I screamed his name with sheer ecstasy as my warm juices coated his fingers.

As I came down from my explosive orgasm, I could feel the light lift of my hips and the tender kisses along my inner thigh as Peter placed my legs over his shoulder. With a deep thrust, he entered me, giving me what I needed and desired for so long. Driving his cock deeper inside, I felt the onset of another orgasm. That, right then, was all I needed. I never wanted to be without it, or him. I knew that I loved this man's heart, body, and soul. I began to shudder; my body belonged to only him. I felt his escape, his body's release from the last couple of days spilled into me as my walls tightened around him. He was home, I was home.

Peter surprised me with the most unbelievable breakfast that I had ever consumed. Having my meal in bed had to be one of the most romantic things a guy had ever done for me. God, how I loved this man. As I finished the last of my meal, I heard the water running in the bathroom and guessed that Peter was drawing a bath for me. When he returned, there was a look of contentment on his face. I had never seen this look before. Sliding in beside me, he wrapped his arms around my body and pulled me closer. Something had changed in him. Raising my head, I looked into his beautiful eyes. "Peter, is something wrong?" I asked, placing my hand on his chest.

"Far from it, baby. I have never felt so free. Everything that has happened with you and with me has been like a vise getting tighter and tighter. When I found out that you had been taken, I thought my world ended, just when I thought everything was finally going our way. I never want to have that feeling again. I love you so much, Lilly, that my heart sings every time you're near me."

Taking his hand in mine and crossing my fingers over his, I lowered my lips to his and said, "I love you too, Peter. I have never met a man who has given me what you have. I think that I have always loved you, but was afraid to admit it to myself."

Peter flipped me over and lowered his head to mine. His kiss was filled with love and compassion. "I better get you in the bath, otherwise I won't ever want to leave this bed," he said.

~\*\*\*\*~

Over the next several weeks, Peter and I spent more and more time together at his place. My condo was a constant reminder of how my privacy was invaded. After Peter told me about Pierre and what he did, I no longer felt safe knowing that he could get to me the way he did. Peter suggested that I sell the condo and move in with him. I loved his place in Jersey City. Even though it was further away from my gallery, I loved the morning commute with him to Manhattan. He still insisted on protecting me. Cop and the other guys checked on me daily, making sure I was okay. Cop came around the gallery the most. I wasn't convinced that checking up on me was the only reason he stopped by every day. I had a sneaky suspicion that something was going on between him and Brie.

Peter, too, would stop in at the gallery, giving me a little something extra on his visits. Every day I spent with this man, I gave him more of my heart. I knew he was the man I would spend the rest of my life with. We fit together perfectly. There were no more secrets. We never talked more about my brother or what happened that day in the treehouse. I later found out that my mom's choices took away her freedom. She was sentenced to ten years in jail. I thought about visiting her, but I could never bring myself to go. I had everything I needed or ever wanted right here. I had loving parents, a wonderful friend who was more of a sister to me, and a man who loved me more than life itself.

I had my everything. I had a wonderful home, a job that I loved, the life I always dreamed of. But most of all, I had Peter, and he had me.

## About the Author

A. L. Long lives in Greeley, Colorado sharing a home with her wonderful husband and granddaughter. When she isn't reading or writing, she enjoys spending time with friends. She also enjoys her morning jogs and family weekend outings. Out of everything, she most enjoys driving in her little two-seater convertible with the top down which she received from her gorgeous husband of twenty-one years.

I hope you found Hewitt enjoyable to read. Please consider taking the time to share your thoughts and leave a review on the on-line bookstore. It would make the difference in helping another reader decide to read this and my upcoming collection to the Jagged Edge Series.

To get up–to-date information on when the next Jagged Edge Series will be released click on the following link http://allong6.wix.com/allongbooks and add your information to mailing list. There is also something extra

# Also by A. L. Long

## Shattered Innocence

Next to Never: Shattered Innocence Trilogy

Next to Always (Book Two): Shattered Innocence Trilogy

Next to Forever (Book Three): Shattered Innocence Trilogy

## Jagged Edge Series

Hewitt: Jagged Edge Series #1

## Coming Soon!!!!!!

Cop: Jagged Edge Series #2

# To keep up with all the latest releases:

## Twitter:

https://twitter.com/allong1963

## Facebook:

http://www.facebook.com/ALLongbooks

## Official Website:

https:/www.allongbooks.com

Made in United States
Troutdale, OR
04/07/2025

30375533R00194